Sheila Kumar is an independent writer and editor based in Bangalore. She worked for the Times of India Group in Bangalore and Delhi, then at *Femina*, Delhi for over a dozen years before turning freelancer. Her books include a collection of short stories *Kith and Kin*; *Chronicles of a Clan*, *No Strings Attached* and *A Gluten-free Life* (as co-author).

Our Start-up Affair

SHEILA KUMAR

SPEAKING
TIGER

SPEAKING TIGER PUBLISHING PVT. LTD
4381/4, Ansari Road, Daryaganj
New Delhi 110002

Copyright © Sheila Kumar 2019

Published in India by Speaking Tiger in paperback in 2019

ISBN: 978-93-88874-06-9
eISBN: 978-93-88326-91-9

10 9 8 7 6 5 4 3 2 1

Typeset in Adobe Devanagari by Jojy Philip, New Delhi

For…
Gee, the quintessential Bangalore girl;
Nitu, the once and future Bangalore girl;
Renu, who has her own Bangalore memories.

CHAPTER ONE

This guy. Hottest thing I've seen. All day. All month. All year. Drool. Aditi messaged her friend, not bothering to hide her smile as she looked down at the glow of her cellphone.

Ritu's reply was not long in coming. Whowhowho?

Aditi hesitated, then hit the keys on her cellphone.

Actually, he's driving the share cab I'm in. Am sitting up front. Next to him.

After sending the message, in a purely reflex action Aditi shot a sidelong glance at the man she'd been drooling over. He glanced casually at her and once again Aditi felt her pulse racing just looking into his dark eyes. Instinctively she gave him a smile, deep dimples appearing on both cheeks. He looked startled for a moment, then smiled back and the smile fairly demolished an already vulnerable Aditi.

Hot, hot, hot, Aditi thought blissfully to herself, then quickly shared that sentiment with Ritu.

Sorry to sound like a total snob. But you are leching over a cabbie? Ritu replied promptly.

If this guy is a cabbie, I'll…I'll…I'll give up vodka shots for a month. Six months. A year. Aditi texted back wildly. This man didn't look anything like the cabbies who usually drove her from place A to place B—no, not in a month of Sundays. It wasn't just the way he looked, though the way he looked was really easy on the eye. He had a head of thick hair. He had fine, chiselled features, an aquiline nose, gorgeously shaped lips and The. Most. Sexy jawline ever. Aditi was a connoisseur of jawlines; her friends were vastly amused by the fact that she first looked at a man's jawline, then decided if he was hot or not. The jawline she was surreptitiously ogling now was faintly shadowed with stubble and really called for long feminine fingers to run over it, softly, caressingly. Aditi's fingers. Her breath quickened.

But good looks apart, here was the thing: this man seemed like he was driving the cab as some sort of a hobby. The moment this thought crept into Aditi's mind, she stifled a giggle. Who drove cabs for a hobby?

In the meantime, a fresh fight broke out between the mother and teenaged son in the back of the cab and Aditi was quickly reminded just why she was sitting up front with the driver. She was sharing the cab with a family of three, one of them sitting in defeated silence while the other two, mother and son, were going hammer and tongs at each other. There was no way anyone in the vehicle could miss out on the finer details of the fight. The boy wanted to apprentice with a filmmaker and his mother saw it as a gateway to all sorts of venal vices, all of which she was listing out loud. They had been arguing all the way from Jakkasandra and while Aditi had been rooting silently for the boy at first, now she was plain bored of this family's affairs. *Shut up already*, she wanted to shout.

Aditi lived in Tippasandra and that was still quite some distance, much gridlocked traffic and many potholed roads away. Hey, was that a trace of fragrance wafting her way from the man sitting beside her? She leaned towards him as unobtrusively as possible to investigate the matter further.

The driver turned his head to look at her.

'Something the matter?' he asked. In unaccented, perfect English. And, catching her expression, grinned that devastating grin again.

'Er, no,' Aditi replied, wondering wildly if she could follow that up with, 'I was just wondering, what is your name?'

Even as she opened her mouth to start a conversation with this hunk because who knew when such an opportunity would arise again, the mother proclaimed loudly from the back seat, 'In fact, you might be better off becoming a driver like the man driving us, Bunty!'

Aditi opened her large, brown eyes wide, shooting the driver a curious look, even as Bunty groaned 'Ma!' in total embarrassment. The head of that household folded into himself further.

Maybe the driver hadn't heard? Because not a muscle moved in his face, or around that amazing jawline. Then, he said to Aditi *sotto voce*, 'Actually, it's not such a bad job at all.' She burst out laughing. A hunk with a sense of humour—not bad at all. Her suspicions about this man being a true-blue cabbie deepened. He had such an air of quiet confidence about him. Who *was* this guy?

The outburst by the angry woman shifted the dynamics of the argument in the back seat for the remainder of the journey and a fraught, loaded silence descended till the cab reached Indiranagar and the family got off. Aditi caught the hapless Bunty's eye and gave him a cheerful thumbs-up. This was intercepted by the mother who glared suspiciously at her.

When the cab started again, Aditi said with a gurgle of laughter, 'Now she thinks I was hitting on her Bunty!'

'Poor Bunty,' the driver said in a deep voice laced with amusement. 'Do you want to go sit at the back now?' he asked.

'No. Why?' Aditi was startled. 'I live just five minutes away.'

Did he think she was a snob? Or had he caught her leaning towards him and felt uncomfortable with such blatant flirting? With those looks, with the kind of quiet confidence he exuded, didn't he have women passengers hitting on him? Hard to believe he didn't. Aditi often got into conversations with the drivers of the cabs she took and she had interacted with sweet cabbies, earnest cabbies, surly cabbies, inarticulate cabbies. But sadly enough, she couldn't remember the last time she'd met a cabbie like this one. If he *was* a cabbie.

'Oh, it's just that there's all that space, in case you want it.' His voice was suave, smooth. Deciding to let that comment pass Aditi asked, 'This is a new cab company, isn't it? It's the first time I've taken a cab from Caboyea.' And then struck by a new thought, she impetuously told him, 'But I think that's one hell of a corny name for a cab service. Tell your bosses that.'

The driver opened his mouth to say something, then seemed to think the better of it. Smiling politely he said, 'Yes, it's a new company, just started a few months ago. But it's doing very well, thank you.'

Before Aditi knew it, she had fallen for the bait. 'I didn't ask,' she informed him in all seriousness before realizing she'd been had.

'Yes, I know,' his lips were quaking with suppressed laughter. 'I just thought you might like to know how Caboyea is doing.'

Super-hot. And funny with it, Aditi thought dreamily but had no time to expand on that since they'd turned into the Tippasandra main road and she needed to guide him down the smallest lane ever, to her block of flats.

He helped set her outsized bag on the pavement but much to

her disappointment, didn't ask her anything or try to prolong the conversation. She thanked him, registering the lean taut body that went—and went so well—with that amazing face. How on earth was she going to ask him for his contact details? Even as she was frantically thinking up a strategy, he got back into the car, raised one hand in a casual bye and was gone. Just like that.

There was only one thing for it: whine to Ritu. Which was what Aditi was doing minutes after she entered the apartment she shared with the other girl.

'He was soooo cute,' Aditi said. 'Tall, dark, handsome.' She settled comfortably onto the yak-skin rug that had been her father's gift to this small flat. A slightly ridiculous gift, way too large for a space where you couldn't swing a cat, even if you were cruel enough to want to swing a cat. It was a heavy, black, hairy rug that was impossible to match with any kind of colour accent in the living room.

'Yeah,' said Ritu laconically. 'And a cabbie.'

'Shut up, you insufferable snob. How about when you were crushing on that guy who peddled DVDs outside City Shoppe?' Aditi retorted, throwing a cushion at her friend, who caught it neatly and characteristically tucked it away to one side.

'Don't try to finger me, Addy; I did *not* have a crush on that fellow. I just said he had the most amazing eyes ever, that's all,' Ritu informed her solemnly.

'Actually, I think this man is not really a cabbie,' Aditi cocked her head to one side, as she gave the matter further thought. 'There was something about him. Also, he was wearing a nice open-collared shirt and…was it faded jeans? Yes, he was wearing jeans. Don't they have to wear some sort of uniform? Well, he wasn't wearing one. Which means…'

'Which means he's a rich dude who paid off the real cabbie the moment he set eyes on you, the future love of his life,' Ritu was now laughing like a jackass. 'And he did that just so he could get to know where you live and can start to stalk you.'

'That,' Aditi said beatifically, 'is the sweetest thing anyone has said to me.' This shut Ritu up, for all of five seconds. Aditi stuck her tongue out at her friend and the girls went into the kitchen to get their dinner, prepared by Ritu tonight and consisting of spaghetti with roast peppers and an avocado salad.

Ritu, as she herself often proclaimed loudly and defensively, was no cook. Aditi was. But tonight the spaghetti, though more al dente than was ideal, wasn't too bad. Ritu had kept a bottle of their favourite rosé on standby and both girls poured liberally from it. John Legend, a particular favourite with Ritu, played in the background, with the noise of the falling water in the mini fountain competing for attention. Aditi detested the water fountain but Ritu's mother believed in vaastu as well as in everything her family astrologer told her. And the astrologer had told her that the apartment needed the sound of continually falling water to alleviate the inherent dangers two young women living together could and would face. Aditi had had a tough time keeping a straight face and keeping her decidedly unruly tongue in check on hearing that but she was quite fond of Ritu's mother, so there it was in the corner of the dining section, the stupid water fountain unit. Also, the flat belonged to Ritu's parents and they had first say in matters like these.

The girls had been living here for two years now and though it was a longish commute to work for Ritu, as opposed to just a ten minutes' walk for Aditi, they had grown quite fond of the apartment. It was full of light for most of the day. Home decoration had to of necessity be eclectic, what with water fountains and yak-skin rugs coexisting with Toda embroidered throws, an ancient divan from Aditi's grandmother's house in Kerala, and two—just two—walls painted a Mediterranean terracotta red. The girls often had friends and office colleagues over, and the adda was a big hit in their circles.

'How are your uncle and aunt doing?' Ritu asked.

'They are doing fine. They were happy to have me help them settle into the new place. I think Prema aunty is a bit troubled that it's so far from town, though.'

'There is no place that's too far from the centre of Bangalore any longer,' Ritu said.

'True that,' Aditi agreed. 'In any case, the two of them don't any longer relish coming into town often. Uncle can't handle the traffic, poor man. And once the little garden in front of their unit comes up, I think both of them will like life in Jakkasandra. They have nice neighbours, I met some of them in the four days I was there. It's a very nice retirement community, actually.'

She added, 'And oh, Prema aunty has sent dessert for you.'

'Her light-as-air chocolate cake?' Ritu asked eagerly.

'Yup!'

'Well, go on and bring it to the table then. I have an early start tomorrow.' Ritu Hegde was a graphic designer who was always rushing about clutching brightly coloured folders with sheafs of paper that stuck out and threatened to spill out any time, a ballpoint pen stuck in her glossy bun, her toenails and lipstick always a deep matching scarlet. She made an arresting picture and Aditi often voiced her suspicion that Ritu's bosses hired her purely for decorative purposes, only to get poked viciously each time by the same pen in Ritu's tresses which obviously had manifold uses.

Ritu worked for the city's top graphic firm. The two girls had been friends from their high school days, had fought, fallen out, made up and promised eternal fealty—basically remained good friends for more years than they cared to count.

Aditi now remembered that she too had to meet a client first thing in the morning. It was early days in her new business and that meant much legwork, not that she grudged a moment of it. Once the start-up really started up and got running, Aditi and the team could relax and—fingers crossed—look to actually making profits. Till then, it was all about artful pitches and presentations, faithfully delivering on promises, tight-as-hell budgets, some scrimping and saving, some cab and auto rides, many Metro rides, and a whole lot of fun.

The girls demolished half of the large cake at a rapid speed interspersed with many sounds of appreciation, and then decided to retire to bed.

Just at the door of her room, Aditi turned to Ritu and told her firmly, 'From now on, I will use only Caboyea.' Then she shut the door on Ritu's cackle of laughter.

CHAPTER TWO

Aditi slept like a rock as she always did and if a chiselled jawline crept into her dreams, it had faded to a pleasant glow by the time she got up. One thing fell sharp and clear into her mind though: she needed to scroll down the numbers in her phone and find *that* 'driver's' contact details. It would be the last number dialled. What are you going to do after you find out his number, the voice of her good angel asked her warily. Nothing, she told it airily, I just want to know. That's all.

The grin wiped itself out when she found the cab details on her cellphone screen. Because while the description of the car was right, there was no way the driver details fit. Apparently a Raj KS had been her driver and the earnest face of the moustachioed man on the thumbnail pic was most certainly *not* the hunk who had driven Bunty, his parents and Aditi to their respective homes last evening. This was someone else. Intense disappointment fought with curiosity in Aditi's brain. Oy! This was a crime, right, driving under an assumed name?

She had no time to ponder this strange matter, though, given that she was running late for work. However, Aditi generally behaved like a whirlwind once she was up and as always she was ready in ten minutes, all set to grab a hurried breakfast and leave for her office. A casual glance in the mirror showed her what she took for granted but many others appreciated: a trim figure, short enough to be forever called petite, a mass of silken curls currently coloured a deep shade of auburn shot with pink, a pair of large expressive eyes the colour of hazelnut cappuccino, the smallest diamond pin glistening on the side of a shapely nose, and Botticelli lips. The last feature was a major irritant to Aditi though many an enamoured man threatened to write odes to those very lips.

She nearly always wore long skirts, gaily patterned, block-printed, in earthy colours, and paired them with short tops, camis, kurtis and kurtas; today she was airing out a deep red skirt paired with a beige sleeveless top. Loads of silver bangles and dangling silver arrowhead earrings completed the picture.

'Lookin' good, girl,' she told her reflection cheerfully and shot off to get some breakfast. Ritu had left fast-congealing cooked cereal on the dining table and Aditi quickly re-heated it, sliced a banana into it and wolfed it down standing. Then she was out of the door.

Her workplace was a mere ten-minute walk away and Mickey was at his desk when she entered the studio loft that served as their office. They had painted the place themselves in a pleasing shade of soft yellow, which they noticed went well with the most crotchety clients. Not that they got too many crotchety clients, thank heavens. Pia Dasgupta and Raman Kumar, the other two who made up the full complement of their core team, had yet to make an appearance.

Aditi and Mickey, whose real name was Chandan Bhatia, had started their business together last year. The Snack Team brought those who were looking for out-of-the-ordinary snacks together with chefs, both professional as well as homemakers, who cooked up these snacks. Just a few months ago they had widened their database and now supplied short eats as well as chefs for catered events across Bangalore. Aditi and Mickey handled the business and tech end of things while Pia, a whiz at accounting, did the math and Raman, who had studied at the Culinary College of America, was the food man. On paper, those were their given designations but on the ground all four of them crossed over, involved themselves in every aspect of the business and worked as a tight unit. It was hard work but all of them were committed to this baby, the Snack Team. In between, they managed to have fun, too.

Mickey cocked a mobile eyebrow and surveyed Aditi keenly. 'You are er…glowing today,' he said, lips slanted in a sardonic grin. 'Wassup?'

'I always glow,' Aditi informed her burly friend loftily.

'You wish! No, it's something else. Wassup and spill!'

And Aditi found herself telling Mickey, her classmate in college, her closest friend apart from Ritu, all about last evening's cab journey and about the 'cabbie' too.

'He was divine,' she sighed, trailing off, her eyes going all soft and dreamy.

Then Mickey said, 'Mmm. Cab driver.' And even as Aditi glared across at him, he hurriedly finished his sentence: 'No, really, good show!'

'Good show?' Aditi gaped.

'Yup,' Mickey told her firmly. 'We need a cabbie on call in our business.'

Just as Aditi was about to turn the air blue with cussing, and she did an effective line in cussing, first Pia then Raman walked in and the conversation turned to work.

'The kitchen people said they could meet our quantity and time deadlines without any problem,' reported Raman briskly. Then he added, 'But.'

'Ah, what would we do if there were no buts,' drawled Mickey not in the least perturbed. Aditi glowered at him and gently prompted Raman: 'But?'

'But we need to beef up our transport quota. We just don't have enough people to pick up the stuff, drop it off, ferry it across Bangalore,' Raman ended with an almost triumphant flourish. Not too surprising because he'd been haranguing them to add to their delivery staff for ages now. The Snack Team had been tackling this delivery-logistics versus client-perceptions problem for a while now, and a working solution was still nowhere in sight. However, this quartet was nothing if not optimistic and was sure they'd crack it, sooner or later.

Pia stepped in, saying softly but firmly, 'No, we can't hire more people, we don't have the money for that. When we started, it was with the clear intention that we'd only ferry food within a tight parameter...five kilometres, right? Then we thought we could handle a larger fleet, so we pushed that limit. But we have to call a halt somewhere. We'll have to work on rerouting and maximization of existing resources with the team we have.'

There settled a thoughtful silence which was suddenly broken. 'I know a driver,' Mickey piped up and all three of them turned expectantly to him.

'Well, I don't,' he said with a wicked grin. 'But Aditi does...'

'No, I don't,' Aditi told Pia and Raman who had turned to look at her hopefully. 'This is Mickey's Monday morning wit.' She gave him a look full of threat. An unmoved Mickey guffawed but mercifully fell silent. And then the four of them set to ironing out the transport problem before Aditi rushed off for the first client meeting of the day.

~

It was a good thing that Aditi didn't have too much time to think about the good-looking cabbie much all of that week. She did find herself in Caboyea vehicles at least twice and her drivers were polite to a fault, drove competently, got her to her destination on time, but they were not *him*. She wildly considered asking if they knew a tall dude in his late twenties with a very straight nose and a seductive jawline but rather regretfully decided against it. The fact that she had even considered asking was evidence of the unbridled side to her that her mother was forever warning her about. What's more, she was near-obsessing over an impersonator, too! That man sure wasn't the Raj KS listed on the site!

And so it was that she dialled for a Caboyea car after a night of clubbing just off MG Road late on a Saturday night. She was beginning to like this cab service; their vehicles were clean, their drivers nice and polite, at least so far, so she was a happy experiencer.

It was pouring cats and dogs and of course, Aditi didn't have an umbrella to hand; who took umbrellas to parties anyway? As she slid into the cab, carefully manoeuvring her orange silk skirt into the vehicle, a familiar voice asked, 'Drop-off point, Tippasandra?'

Mouth suddenly dry and heart racing, Aditi Pillai looked up and into a pair of midnight black eyes. 'Hi,' she said huskily.

'Hi,' he returned casually, shooting her a friendly smile even as his eyes took in the very pretty picture she made. She registered the look and frantically wondered if her lipstick had faded away, if her cat's-wing eyeliner still held good after many hours of partying, if her bra straps were staying out of sight like all good bra straps ought to do unless they were meant not to.

And then Aditi being Aditi, she found herself saying, 'Long time no see. How have you been?'

The man laughed, a deep-throated very amused laugh that instantly got her toes curling in their sky-high stilettoes. 'I've been good,' he told her. 'And you?'

And just like that, the two of them got talking, easily, casually, the chat flowing from the back seat to the driver's seat, and back again to her. They talked of the weather, of course. Bangalore had received very little rain all this monsoon and things boded ill for the city's water supply. They talked of the city's appalling roads, and even more appalling traffic. All the while, he was manoeuvring the cab through the inevitable weekend logjams, made a hundred times worse by the heavy rain. At times, they were crawling but Aditi had absolutely no complaints. She had no problem at all if the two of them were stuck in this cab for a long, long time.

From time to time, the streetlights would throw his profile into sharp relief for her to admire, then cast it back into darkness. Every time he changed gears, the muscles in his forearm would flex in a way that totally turned her on. 'Music?' he asked and she nodded happily. The strains of a plaintive guitar filled the confines of the cab. He'd switched on a rock FM station. *Man with good taste*, Aditi thought happily.

Idiot girl, a voice inside her head spoke suddenly. *Introduce yourself. Or else, all is in vain!*

'Oh, I'm Aditi Pillai, by the way,' she said and saw his lips quirk with hidden amusement. Did he find her name funny, she wondered indignantly.

'Hello, Aditi Pillai,' he intoned solemnly. 'Sorry I can't offer you my hand, I need both of them on the wheel just now.' And Aditi's truant mind immediately conjured up a most interesting scenario where he was putting those long-fingered hands of his to very good use in different ways. *Aditi!* her good angel gasped in prissy fashion. *I can't help it,* she told the creature sulkily. *He's sexy AF.*

'And you are?' she asked, sticking to the point despite the diversions being put in her way by her mischievous mind.

'I am...? Oh, yes. I'm Raj.' His voice was pleasant, his tone even.

Aditi stared at the back of his head in shocked silence. Liar! No, you are not, she wanted to shout. But that would expose her interest, make her seem like a stalker, so she held her peace, swallowed her disappointment.

He was obviously involved in some resource replacement scam, she decided. Perhaps Raj KS was his best friend and was now laid up in hospital? Perhaps Raj KS was on holiday in Sri Lanka earning some much deserved downtime and this man was standing in for him, doing his good deed for the month? Perhaps Raj KS was in jail for impersonating some other driver of this dashed cab company and this man was now standing in for him... by impersonating him! Aditi knew her imagination was going into overdrive but what the hell, this situation was so weird!

Whatever. The point was, this guy was not Raj KS. Then again, she couldn't really believe that he was up to no good despite the fake name. No one with a jawline like that, she mused...

'Been working for Caboyea for long?' she asked, striving to sound like it was just an off-the-cuff question.

'Yes,' he told her. 'Ever since the cab company started operations.'

Aditi's unruly tongue ran away with her again. 'What were you doing before that?' she asked, then bit her lip. Had she come off sounding like she was putting down his job? So not good, Aditi.

But he answered easily, not seeming offended in the least. 'Before that I was studying for my business administration degree.'

This time Aditi masked her surprise though, truth be told, she was no longer really surprised by anything this man, this faux Raj KS, told her. Which was why she found herself nodding in quiet accord when he followed that up with…'at Urbana Champaign. In Illinois.'

'I know Urbana Champaign,' Aditi told him with a bright smile which he couldn't see. 'My brother is an U of I alumni. He loved it, and when I went visiting, I fell in love with the place, too. All that greenery, the campus so well laid out…'

He didn't ask about her brother. 'But you didn't apply to study there?' he asked instead, his tone devoid of anything but an off-hand casual interest.

'No. I went to JNU instead.'

'Ah,' he said on a smile. It was a smile that held something besides pleasant amusement.

'What?' Aditi asked and he shrugged.

'No, what?' she insisted.

'Well, you look a JNU girl. The billowing skirts, nose-pin, jholas, and all that jazz.' He shot her a purely wicked look in the rear-view mirror, then said, '…quite the sexiest look ever.' OMG. Her cabbie was flirting with her!

She chose to be mollified by that last statement. 'Jhola? I'll have you know I'm carrying an It bag,' she told him sarcastically, then followed it up with, 'Oh boy, a prejudiced cabbie.' He threw his head back and laughed.

The conversation then moved to music, and they discovered they both had a rather old-fashioned taste in music since they loved rock and jazz and detested EDM and trance. In the meantime, the rains lessened, then stopped, the traffic thinned a bit, then was back four-deep on the roads of Indiranagar. 'Not one jazz act worth its name has performed here in Bangalore, not one Jazz Yatra,' he said ruefully and she nodded her head so hard, it was in danger of falling off, not that he could see it from the front seat.

'How come you didn't join Ola or Uber, the more established companies, I mean?' Aditi asked with genuine curiosity.

He opened his mouth to say something, then seemed to think the better of it and closed his mouth again. Their eyes met in the rear-view mirror and Aditi raised her well-shaped eyebrows in query.

'I prefer start-ups,' he said flatly. 'Less baggage, more streamlined, and with more potential to live up to its potential.'

Aditi laughed, her dimples flashing deep. It was his turn to raise his eyebrows.

'Nothing,' she told him and his face seemed to close. *Whoa, he thinks I'm snubbing him*, Aditi thought with a pang.

They had reached her place. As she got down, Aditi said with a smile, 'Actually, I totally got what you said about start-ups. I work for a start-up, too. My own. Well, it's a company I co-own.'

Now she had his full attention.

'Really,' he said. 'What is it called?'

'The Snack Team,' she told him. 'We see to the short-eats needs of people and businesses.'

He came back smoothly, without missing a beat. 'The Snack Team! What a clichéd name.'

She started to reply indignantly then caught his teasing smile and trailed off. Switching gears, she told him, 'We are quits then, working for companies with terrible names.'

'I didn't say it was terrible, only clichéd,' he protested and even as she stood by the kerb, hoping like hell he'd ask what she was doing tomorrow, he lifted one hand in farewell like the last time and eased the car carefully out of the narrow lane. She kept looking but he didn't for even a moment catch her eye in the side-view mirror.

Damn, Aditi thought, then brightened. *I'll find him on social media*, she thought happily. Except, when she tried she just couldn't find him. On any social media platform. All the Rajs out there—and the online world seemed full of Rajs—were all different men. Plump-cheeked Rajs, moustachioed Rajs, goatee-bearded Rajs, bald Rajs, a couple of Rajs with 70s-style sideburns, one Raj with an eyebrow ring. Men she didn't want to befriend at all.

'What next?' Ritu asked laconically as the two girls sat finishing the last of some wine they had in the fridge and listening to Arijit Singh on loop. Given their busy schedules, they cherished these downtime segments.

Aditi slanted a wicked dimpled smile at her friend. 'I went to a school whose motto was Never Give Up.'

'Okay,' Ritu said, raising a hand to forestall any further declaration of intent. 'I get it. Just keep me updated.'

'For sure, woman, for sure,' Aditi assured her, laughing.

And late at night, just before Aditi closed her book and stretched a hand out to switch off the bedside lamp, her phone pinged. It was a message.

'*What's an it bag, anyway?*' read the question.

Aditi laughed, stored the number under 'Fake Raj,' then plumped her many pillows and settled down to sleep. Ha! Now that they had made contact, the answer could wait, she thought. She didn't want to come off seeming needy. In fact, why was she even contemplating some sort of friendship with a man whose real name she didn't know? On that profound thought, she slid into her usual deep, dreamless sleep.

CHAPTER THREE

Aditi never got around to telling him what an It bag was. Him, that's how she thought of him. Not Raj. Never Raj. *Maybe I should give him another name, one I think suits him better*, she thought with amusement. *Fraud aadmi*, scoffed her good angel and since Aditi was eccentric enough to often talk back to these angels of hers, she replied spiritedly: *Hey! It's just a matter of time before I get to the root of this fake-name business.*

Anyway, the reason she forgot to get back to him was a sudden crisis at the Snack Team. Against all expectations, it had nothing to do with the delivery problem they were trying to get on top of, it was a complaint about a large consignment of coriander-spiced kachoris which the client insisted tasted stale. Mickey and Aditi were the official troubleshooters of the company, so they hared off to Whitefield and poof! went the day in mollifying the irate client, promising an immediate make-good (in the form of coriander kodubale, Karnataka's own chakli), while Raman rushed to the concerned food kitchen delving into just what had gone wrong. Stale ingredients, a careless cook, these were things they just couldn't afford, not now, not later.

The whole affair took up the next few days and it was Thursday before the four of them could really relax, taking comfort in the knowledge that they had plugged all the holes and ensured such a thing wouldn't happen again. Smoothing the cracks over, as well as the long harrowing commutes from Indiranagar to Whitefield, had been an exhausting business for Aditi and Mickey.

'This is the part about running the business that I hate the most,' announced Pia sanctimoniously. It was late, they were still in the office but had called in for kathi rolls and Coke. There was some beer in the office fridge but no takers for them tonight.

'What?' Aditi asked automatically, running a hand through her curls and pressing two fingers to one temple.

'This client appeasement,' Pia replied. 'It's a tough job, smoothing ruffled feathers.'

There was an electric silence and Pia, always slow to wake up to the mood, finally looked up. 'What?' she asked in all innocence.

Mickey was spluttering. 'Client appeasement? Pia Dasgupta, you money-cruncher, what client appeasement did you do?'

Pia was unfazed. 'I know you did it, Mickey, you and Aditi,' she said, tucking a swathe of hair tinted a deep blue behind one shell-like ear. 'It's just that listening to how you went about it is giving me a headache. I have a…'

'Yes, we know,' Mickey told her dryly, his tone laced with affection though. 'A delicate temperament. You tell us about it all the time.'

'Dude, lay off her,' Raman said with a wry smile. Aditi caught Mickey's eye and winked. She'd been telling Mickey for a while now that Raman was showing a marked interest in the lovely Pia who, of course, was sublimely oblivious to it. That was the appealing thing about their Pia, she coasted through life entirely and inoffensively absorbed in herself and never noticed anything beyond her pretty upturned nose. However, she was a dab hand at finance, with a natural flair for math and accountancy.

Now she said to Aditi brightly, 'Hey Aditi! I never got to show you what I scored at the Leather Shop a couple of days ago.' And out came a lovely nappa-leather beige handbag with oversized grommets. Not quite what Aditi would have spent her own hard-earned money on but very much up Pia's street.

Mickey and Raman rolled their eyes and fell to scarfing down their just delivered food without ceremony.

'Looks a real It bag, doesn't it?' Pia asked happily and that's when Aditi remembered.

'Oh damn!' she wailed loudly, startling the guys. 'I forgot to tell him about the It bag!'

The quick-witted Mickey caught on immediately and raised a mocking eyebrow which Aditi took no notice of. Raman asked 'What?' and after the regulation pause, so did Pia.

'Oh, my boyfriend wanted to know what an It bag was,' Aditi told them airily, quite enjoying the look on their faces.

'You have a new boyfriend and never told me?' Pia squealed. 'Who is he?'

'He's a driver,' Mickey intoned solemnly.

'An F1 driver? Ooooh, how exciting! I wanna meet him,' Pia exclaimed, actually clapping her hands with excitement. Conversations with Pia often went just like this.

'An F1 driver based in Bangalore?' asked a puzzled Raman.

Aditi rolled her eyes at an unrepentant Mickey but refused to say anything. 'I gotta get in touch with him now,' she patiently explained to Pia. 'I'll fill you in on all details later.'

Just calling him her boyfriend gave Aditi a thrill, a foolish thrill. Except, her boyfriend, whatever his name was, just didn't pick up the phone.

Aditi tried a couple of times later that night too, then settled for a message.

Hi, was caught up with crazy-crazy at work. Sup?

And then days passed, the weekend came and went with absolutely no response from him. Belatedly, Aditi realized her silence at the start of the week could have been misconstrued as a cold shoulder. Like she'd had second thoughts about hobnobbing with a driver and all that.

Damn. But surely he wasn't that insecure a person? Then again, what did she know about the man anyway? He could well be a very insecure person.

Now that things were somewhat smooth at work again, Aditi realized she was kind of crushing on the cute cabbie. Which was why, when the next week she got into a Caboyea taxi, checked the back of the cabbie's head and discerned that it was not 'her boyfriend,' she was so disappointed that it took her a full minute to get a hold of herself. Then the man turned around to confirm her drop-off destination, and she found she was looking at Raj KS. The man whose thumbnail photo she had seen on her phone, all those days ago.

'Tippasandra,' she affirmed huskily. As the cab set into motion, she hurriedly checked her phone. Same cab, same name, different man.

'Er, your name is Raj? Raj KS?' Even though she tried hard to sound casual, her voice must have betrayed something because the driver sounded distinctly nervous.

'Yes, ma'am,' he said politely. 'Is something wrong?'

Aditi had had enough.

'Then who,' she demanded testily just like her high school teacher, 'is the other Raj KS?'

There was silence for a beat, during which she saw in the rear-view mirror that the man was looking decidedly shifty.

Then he said, his voice coming out rather like a bleat, 'Which other Raj?'

'You know which other Raj. I took this cab twice before, this very cab, and the driver told me his name was Raj KS. And he most definitely wasn't you.'

At this point, she stopped as she had been speaking in English. And so had he. Just like the other Raj KS, this man too, sounded cultured, his English accent-less. Curiouser and curiouser.

But the driver had managed to collect himself in this time.

'No, ma'am,' he said smoothly. 'You are mistaken.'

Aditi wasn't going to give up that easily.

'You are the only Raj at Caboyea?'

'Yes,' he told her, looking quickly at her, then away.

'And how would you know that? You know all the other drivers at the company?' she demanded.

'It's a small company, started just six months ago,' he said, his voice betraying the smallest quaver. 'Caboyea operates its own fleet of taxis. We have a small team of drivers. It's a small operation.'

And then he quickly leaned forward and switched on FM radio. Shalmali Kholgade crooned *Baby ko base pasand hai*. Raj KS drove looking steadily ahead at the road while Aditi sat and glared at the back of his head throughout the journey. This Raj was a bit older than the other. He was also more handsome in real life than in the thumbnail pic she had scrutinized so hard the other day; handsome but not a patch on the other man. He drove as well as his namesake (*Really*, asked Aditi's wicked angel facetiously. *Who knows what that man's name actually is?*) but more cautiously.

What the hell was happening? What was this Raj scam all about? Was she safe with this Raj? Oh hell, Aditi, she told herself impatiently, now your imagination is running riot. Of course, she was safe. She knew how to take care of herself. If this fellow tried anything, she'd thulp him and thulp him most effectively, given how savage she was feeling at the moment.

~

She wasn't too surprised when, much later that night, her phone pinged and there was a message from 'her boyfriend.'

Hi, sorry for delay in replying, was out of town. Let's meet for a drink?

She gave the phone screen a murderous look. She itched to reply: *I'd happily meet you for a drink…IF I knew just who you were.* Instead, she ignored the message and went back to reading her book. Aditi was a voracious reader who usually dipped into as many as three books at the same time, many of them cookbooks. She'd always preferred reading over television and now, as she switched from a Kindle to a printed book and back quite often, reading remained her favourite leisure occupation. She had actually broken up with her last boyfriend because he had told her loftily on their second date that the movie versions of books were all, without exception, way better than their printed version.

The next few days saw one message arrive every day. **Let's meet for lunch** went one. **Let's meet for dinner** pleaded another. **Let's meet to say hi** asked a third. She refused to reply to the missives, deriving pleasure in being childish.

But she caved in on the fourth day. There was only so long a girl could play hard to get. That too, when the guy was as gorgeous as her cute cabbie.

Alright. When? Where? She texted him back, trying to suppress her excitement.

Late tomorrow? Leave the evening plan to me? Pick you up from your place?

'How?' Ritu asked, agog with curiosity. 'In his cab?'

Aditi caught her friend's eye and went off in a peal of laughter.

'Boy, this has to be a first! For most girls! But I don't care, I'll sit up front,' she assured Ritu.

On Friday evening, when she came back to her flat, Ritu had not returned from work. So, after twenty minutes of standing in front of her skirt-heavy wardrobe, Aditi texted Ritu. What do I wear? The purple skirt? The Sabya knock-off in black and white?

Neither came the reply. You have terrific pins. So, skinny jeans. And remember: get your freak on. Or maybe not, that could be much too much for him to handle.

Ignoring that last bit of gratuitous advice, Aditi dutifully if uncharacteristically, followed her friend's instructions and pulled on a skinnier-than-skinny pair of dark denims and topped that with a lovely peasant top Mickey had got her from a trip he'd taken to Mexico earlier that year. The top was a swirly print of golds, greens, blues and blacks, and in a departure from her usual silverware, she put on just a pair of dangly earrings to match. Also making for a perfect match were the suede boots that hugged her shapely shins lovingly. Eyes deeply kohled-up, a copper-wine lipstick shade on her mouth which made her dusky complexion fairly glow, a spritz of Ralph Lauren's Romance, and Aditi was ready.

Ritu still wasn't back home, which was a pity because Aditi so wanted her to meet the cute cabbie. Then the doorbell rang and she went to answer it with a pounding heart. The moment her eyes fell on him, her first emotion was relief. Relief that she'd opted out of wearing a skirt.

He had a motorbike helmet tucked under one arm and was carrying another one for Aditi. Behind him, on the kerb, stood a sleek black Ducati. Aditi didn't know what she was immediately more thrilled with, the man or his beaut of a bike.

He saw her looking past him at their mode of transport and asked, his voice low and deep, 'Bikes don't hassle you, I hope?'

Aditi shot him such a radiant smile, he looked positively stunned for a second.

'Hassle me? I adore bikes!' She took the helmet from him and adeptly affixed it atop her cascading curls. She saw him looking at her jean-clad legs and hid a smile. *What*, she asked him silently. *You thought those skirts were a disguise for lumpy legs?*

He manoeuvred the high-powered bike carefully out of the small street and onto the main road. Soon, they were on the Whitefield main road and after a while, traffic thinned perceptibly. They also left behind the ubiquitous smell of garbage and petrol fumes that were now an inevitable by-product of Bangalore city. Conversation was pretty well nigh impossible but Aditi didn't want to chat. She was enjoying the bike ride, relishing the cool wind on her face, the feel of his firm waist around which she'd looped her arms casually. And she was right, that elusive fragrance she'd caught that night in his cab *was* his preferred choice of scent. Musky, citrusy, luscious, Aditi decided, leaning in to sniff better.

It was a long ride and then he turned into what looked like a farmhouse. He rode up a driveway lit with old-fashioned globe lights hanging from wrought-iron lampposts. As they drew up at the portico of a sprawling and elegant house, she realized they were at The Homestead, Bangalore's newest, trendiest eatery.

People were already sitting at small trestle tables in the long portico that was the dining area. The colour theme was mint green and sky blue, and complemented the deep green foliage in the surroundings very well. It was a typical balmy Bangalore evening too and the stars shone bright in a navy sky. *What a romantic evening*, thought Aditi with a ripple of amusement. Her companion caught on to her sense of delight and raised an enquiring eyebrow at her. 'Nothing really,' she told him, adding in a prosaic if truthful fashion, 'I'm hungry.'

Later when Ritu asked, Aditi had to think a bit to recall what she'd ordered, what she'd eaten. But she *was* in the food business and was able to tell Ritu about a great Merlot, some delicious lobster and a melt-in-the-mouth risotto. What she had a crystal-clear recall of, though, was the dessert: a mud pie with a thick, gooey centre. She'd scooped up bite after bite enthusiastically, then looked up to see him watching her with a glint in his eye, one that made her heart do a near-vertical jump. They locked glances for a long minute, then she asked huskily, 'What?' And he shook his head, leaned forward and slowly, sensuously, wiped off some chocolate liquid from the corner of her mouth with one finger, the movement a decided caress. Aditi closed her eyes till she felt his finger leave her mouth, then opened them with a sigh and smiled tremulously at him. For once, he didn't smile back.

Much as she hated to admit it to herself, Aditi just needed to look into the dark eyes of the man sitting opposite her and she was lost. They were really eyes she could drown in.

Despite that moment of pure electricity though, they chatted casually, easily. He confessed to an addiction for crime thrillers while she told him of her love for slasher fiction; then they briefly squabbled over the merits of different genres of cinema.

Looking around her, Aditi told him, 'This is such a charming place. I totally get all the hype about it now.'

'I've been here once before,' he replied. 'Someone in my extended family owns the place.'

At which Aditi couldn't resist picking up that particular gauntlet.

'Extended family?' she asked, unwittingly twirling her fork in the air. 'Would that include Raj? Raj KS?'

He didn't miss a beat. 'You mean the real Raj KS?' he asked smoothly.

She gave him a hard look. 'Yes,' she hissed.

'Hey, don't take it so personally,' he said, and there was an apologetic note in his voice. 'He told me about his conversation with you. Raj's my older brother. I stand in for him occasionally.'

'And no one has reported you yet?' she asked with full-on sarcasm.

'It's not a crime, standing in for another driver once in a rare while,' he told her. 'Raj was unwell, now he's back up and running, I mean driving. So Caboyea passengers will now get the real Raj KS.' He smiled at her across the table, clearly turning on the charm offensive.

The effrontery of the man, Aditi fumed to herself, even as she was trying not to notice how his smile threw his sculpted jawline into relief.

Angling her own jaw at him belligerently, she asked, 'Well, considering you are giving me dinner, don't I get to know who you are, Fake Raj?'

Slowly he extended a shapely hand across the table to her. To Aditi's amazement, her hand rose to meet it and in a surreal fashion, they were shaking hands. Both of them seemed equally reluctant to let go of the other's hand.

Then he said, 'Hi, Aditi Pillai. I'm Aditya Shenoy.' And he grinned at her.

Her mouth moved convulsively but she held back the grin that would acknowledge the Aditi-Aditya alliteration.

'Aditya Shenoy,' she said reflectively. 'It's not such a terrible name. Why on earth do you go about pretending to be Raj KS?'

He winced, then leaned forward and picked up her hand which was on the table. Looking deep into her eyes, he said, 'I'm sorry, Aditi. I really am. Family problems dictated that I become Raj for a while. No longer. Now Raj is Raj and I am…Aditya.'

But Aditi was in no mood to let him off the hook that easily. 'So, Aditya Shenoy,' she said, fingers sliding under her jaw in the classic thoughtful pose. 'What is it that you do? Apart from driving your brother's cab?'

'This seems to be a night for revelations. Actually, I own Caboyea,' he said slightly sheepishly but Aditi wasn't in the least surprised and she wasn't going to act surprised either. She had already come to that conclusion a while ago. The math just didn't add up: his U of I degree, his self-confidence, the air of being in charge that he carried with him, the tech phrases he used, all of that somehow didn't fit in with anything less than being the man in the top seat.

No one who spoke the way he did, had the air of authority that sat lightly but definitely on him, who dressed the way he did (today he was wearing a soft leather motorcycling jacket which looked dashed expensive) could be your average cabbie.

'Mmm,' she told him, nodding solemnly though a smile lurked in her eyes. He saw the smile and visibly relaxed. Then he ran a hand reflexively along his jawline and Aditi almost whimpered. That jawline was fast becoming an obsession with her.

However, now that she knew he owned the cab company, there was other stuff she wanted to know.

'The established players giving you a rough time?' she asked him interestedly, then told him, 'The Snack Team had it tough the initial one-and-a-half years, we were fighting off competition of all kinds, big and small, seen and unseen. We started out as a garage start-up literally, our angel investors being our parents. Back then, it was a slog, trying hard for that all-important target of a million hits in six months.'

He listened intently. 'Rivals tried to make you roadkill?' he asked.

'All the bloody time,' she replied. 'Our food entrepreneur competitors sank to disgusting levels to wipe us out. Totally dirty deeds. But we weren't going to go under so easily. We held on grimly, keeping our focus on food, confident that if the product was good the business would fly, the money would come in. I think it's a comment on our quality and staying power that the Snack Team survived, and is now doing quite well for itself.'

She took a deep breath and continued, 'But if there was one thing my partner Mickey and I have learned, it is this: there really is no room for complacency, not in a business that dictates you play the value-adds game and play it deftly, to grow both your awareness levels as well as sales volumes. Kinda like jogging hard to stay in the same place, you know?'

'Yeah, that's right,' he told her, then a spark lit up deep in his eyes. 'There are, at last count, 40,000 cabs on Bangalore's roads. We need to be different. I have put in place a very different business plan for Caboyea. We own and drive our own fleet of cars, as it makes for better control. I want to prove that a small cab company can be run honestly, scrupulously, efficiently, that we can keep clients happy without violating rules, assure them a safe run from pick-up point to destination.'

'How?' asked a curious Aditi.

Aditya then went into details. She listened, marvelling at a plan which seemed simplistic on the surface but was nothing short of ingenious. Suddenly, he broke off and said, 'I've got to tell you something.'

She stared at him. 'What?'

'You know, the second time you travelled in my cab? I kind of arranged that. I was driving past UB City and saw you coming out of the place.'

'You stalked me?' asked Aditi, feigning disapproval. Her eyes gave her away though and Aditya chuckled. 'Hey, that was not stalking. I was just hoping things would go the way I wanted them to. I parked the car some metres ahead and sat waiting, fingers tightly crossed. And hurrah, you called for a Caboyea cab and there I was, the nearest cab in the vicinity.'

'And if I hadn't called for a Caboyea cab?' Aditi asked, tilting her chin provocatively at him.

'If it was meant to happen, it would happen. That's what I told myself as I sat there in the pouring rain.'

Later in the evening, enveloped in a happy silence they walked back to where Aditya had parked his bike. It was late, very late, and there were no other vehicles in the vicinity. When he reached the bike, he turned around, leaning against the gleaming monster and slowly reached for Aditi.

'Aditi. Aditya. Good fit, hey?' he asked her, his voice going down an octave.

Aditi reached out a steady hand and slowly ran it down the side of his face. Aditya took a deep breath. He didn't say anything, just looked steadily at her.

She told him impetuously, 'I've been wanting to do that ever since I met you.'

'Hmmm,' he said gravely, his eyes dancing. 'I've been wanting to do something the moment I set eyes on you, too.'

'What?' Aditi asked, her voice coming out in a squeak despite her best efforts.

'This,' Aditya said, drawing her to him and bending his head.

It was a heavenly kiss and Aditi gave in to the sheer pleasure of kissing him, running her hands over the back of his head. He clamped both arms across her lower waist, held her close to him as he took his time exploring the contours of her mouth, trailing small kisses all along her lips before gently pushing them open. As he deepened the kiss, Aditi found herself clutching his shirt-front, to bring him closer, much closer to her.

Then they broke apart, smiling happily at each other.

'Are you now officially my bae?' Aditi asked teasingly, running the back of her fingers over his chin. There was the faintest of stubble there, she suddenly noticed.

'Are you mine?' Aditya Shenoy asked her, one long finger tucking a strand of her curls behind her ear.

And they sealed the unspoken answer with another kiss.

~

'Wait, wait! I gotta tell you one more thing,' Aditi protested, trying to get Ritu to shut up and listen.

It was the next day, and both girls were not working. They sat at the dining table with the sun pouring in through the French windows, their outsized cups of coffee twirling thin spirals of smoke upwards.

Aditi had told an incredulous Ritu about Aditya's 'coming out,' as it were. At first, Ritu had sat there with her mouth open, then being told unkindly to shut it, she had yelped, 'Come on! This is like some soppy Bollywood movie, a K-Jo one. You mean he really is a rich man?'

'Well, I don't know about that. But hey, he's gotta be richer than us,' Aditi pointed out, giggling madly, then added wickedly, 'And you were right.'

Catching the unholy glee in her friend's face, Ritu asked suspiciously, 'What about?'

'About the reason he pretended to be a cabbie. When he saw me for the second time.'

'No!'

'Yes! He told me.' And she proceeded to tell Ritu.

'Bloody hell!' said a dumbfounded Ritu. 'I don't believe this.'

'Believe it. We were meant to be together. And anyway, you can ask him yourself when you meet him.'

'I will,' Ritu assured her stoutly. But when she did meet Aditya the following Sunday, she didn't ask. Not only that, she appeared to be undergoing some radical transformation and in front of an amused Aditi, went all coy and feminine on Aditya. They clicked immediately, just as Aditi had expected. He asked Ritu about the work she did, she asked him how tough it was to break into a field dominated by the biggies. It seemed to Aditi that they were on the verge of hiring each other after a most satisfactory two-way interview!

'Wtf was that coy Miss Malati act all about?' Aditi asked Ritu when they were alone that night.

'What Miss Malati?' Ritu began to ask in typically aggro fashion, then subsided sheepishly. 'I just felt like pulling one on him. Him being new and all that, he wouldn't have known it wasn't the real me. Know what I mean?'

'Yes,' Aditi told her, giving her the evil eye. 'I do. You were pulling the old one.'

'Did it look fake?' asked Ritu and Aditi chuckled. 'No, silly, it just took me a while to notice you were doing that thing you used to do. Coming over all quivering lips and fluttering eyelashes. Neat job.'

'I just felt like it,' Ritu repeated and they grinned at each other. Ritu often adopted personas she thought it would be fun to take out to parties and dates. It was quite her party trick, as it were. The act didn't last long and when she reverted to being herself, many of her thoroughly unnerved boyfriends often ran from her. Her friends, though, thought these acts were a scream.

Then Aditi shot an enquiring look at her closest friend. Ritu got the import of that look and immediately said, 'He's such a cutie, Addy. Very, very hawt. But is he a keeper?'

Aditi cut in, raising one derisive eyebrow. 'Who is keeping him? I'm dating the man, Ritu Hegde, not adopting him. Or marrying him. I'm having fun, not checking him out as a prospective hubby.'

'Oh yeah,' Ritu said in a reflective manner. 'I forgot just who I was talking to. You won't be tackling him to the ground any time soon, will you?'

'Well, tackling him to the ground sounds a very interesting thing to do, thank you for giving me the idea,' she replied, her eyes twinkling. Both girls burst out laughing.

But Aditi meant what she had told Ritu. Aditya Shenoy was, in one simple word, gorgeous. And he seemed really into her. Therefore, they were going to have heaps of fun getting to know each other, they were going to take each day as it comes and let the future look out for itself. In fact, if the future decided to go get lost for a bit, she would only be too happy. Aditi Pillai did not do commitment. Or marriage, for that matter.

Aditya meeting Mickey was another matter altogether. She had asked him to come up to her office when he came to pick her up after work. And when he did so, Aditi introduced him to Mickey and Pia; Raman wasn't around then.

'Aditya and Aditi. Aditi and Aditya,' Pia kept repeating like it was a haiku she'd just made up. Aditya grinned good-naturedly while Aditi shot Pia an exasperated look.

Mickey was friendly but wary, like a grizzly bear checking out an unknown object. Behind the smile and air of affability, he was observing Aditya keenly, ready to register the smallest step out of line.

But Aditi had realized something about her boyfriend: he was one smooth operator. When on unfamiliar turf, he generally kept his head down, spoke little, observed everything silently and keenly. Now she watched him handle Pia in a friendly fashion while being polite to a fault with Mickey.

'That Kodiak bear in there, is he an ex-boyfriend of yours?' he asked as they went downstairs. Ever since she'd started going out with Aditya, she'd switched to wearing pants, pushed her skirts to the back of her cupboard. She missed her regulation attire but it was no fun going on bike rides if you had to carefully hold down your skirt, and sitting side-saddle was absolutely not an option with her.

Aditi glanced at him to see if the question about Mickey was asked with any baggage but could discern none. He looked curious, that's all.

'Don't call him a Kodiak,' she said automatically then added, 'No, he's not a boyfriend, has never been. But yes, he's a very close friend. We go back a long way together.'

Adiya took the bait. 'How long?' he asked and the question had a territorial ring that pleased her no end. She gave him a potted history of her relationship with Mickey, standing there on the road beside her sexy boyfriend's sexy bike.

'Mmm,' he said, adding, 'That figures. The man is looking out for you and wearing the lookout badge on his sleeve, too.'

'Hell, so?' Aditi retorted. 'That's bad?'

'Not at all,' said Aditya equably. 'I do it on occasion too.'

'You do? Who do you look out for?' she asked, trying not to sound too curious.

'A friend or two. My sister.'

She took a moment to register that. He hadn't talked about his family so far. Neither had he asked her anything about hers. Even the info on Raj KS had been prised out of him.

'You have a sister?' she ventured cautiously.

'Well, sister-in-law, to be precise. She's Raj's…'

'Wife,' finished Aditi for him, grinning like she'd cracked some Megamind quiz. And leaned forward to nuzzle his jaw.

'Aditi, there's an uncle in the next building who is scowling down at you,' he told her laughing.

'He's no uncle, he's our dratted landlord and I don't care,' she said firmly but quickly put her helmet on and swung into place behind him on the bike. Landlords were better appeased, or at least kept in a peaceful state.

Later in bed that night, she asked herself if it really bothered her that Aditya never told her anything about his family. And then she did a quick reality check. Had she told him anything at all about her doctor father, her ad copywriter mother, her beloved brother who'd thrown over a lucrative career in the US to settle down in a Wayanad hamlet and help the tribal communities there? Nope. Even-Steven.

So, the meagre flow of information was not a one-way street. *Hey Addy, it doesn't really bother you and you know that,* she told herself sleepily. She was not a curious creature at the best of times. She took life as it came and most times that worked very well for her. She wasn't going to change for the sake of her cute cabbie now.

CHAPTER FOUR

Aditi floated on a cloud of bliss over the next many months. Being with Aditya Shenoy was good fun, a happy place for her and clearly for him too. Since both of them were perpetually busy, they couldn't meet more often than once a week but they tried to make their dates special. They watched films at their favourite miniplex, they went on to have argumentative dinners after the movie, they hit a lot of pubs, then settled to haunting just the one or two which played good jazz-rock. They tried to eat at every new restaurant that just opened, which was quite a challenge given that Bangalore had new eateries opening just about every other day. Since both of them were not TV-watchers, they skipped the idiot box and did other stuff instead. They went on long rides outside the city limits, where he could open up the Ducati's throttle and let it really rip. Once in a while, he came up to her apartment where they had a cup of coffee with Ritu if she was in.

And yes, they kissed, they nuzzled, they necked but she noticed that Aditya always set the pace; when things started to get really intense, he stepped back. Oh, it was subtle, but Aditi noticed it all the same and wondered at his reticence. If she was lacking in self-esteem, she'd have assumed she didn't turn him on enough. But that was not the case and Aditi knew it. Clearly, there was some other not-very-obvious issue.

But whatever time they could snatch, they spent together. It was not easy; Aditi was busy working on a pitch presentation that Mickey was spearheading and for all his easy-going manner, Mickey was anything but easy-going when it came to work. Aditya too had his hands full with major cab companies, who had a few years' seniority on his fledgling firm, getting into pricing confrontations with the government. He was not for surge-pricing and he definitely was not for padding up the driver roster at the expense of in-depth quality checks, but anyone striking out in a different direction was viewed with immediate suspicion by the others in the field.

'This is crazy,' he told Aditi one evening, running a frustrated hand through his hair, causing it to stand up. 'Cab registrations are now down to almost manageable figures, so we can and should push for quality over quantity. But that's just not happening. These big aggregators play below the radar pretty much most of the time, despite all claims to be sunrise industries. They seek and receive blanket protection. Then when things go wrong, just about everyone in the business gets burned.'

Aditi nodded in total sympathy. There had been a rash of driver-attacks on women passengers over the past fortnight. Ritu herself had got into an unpleasant altercation with a cabbie from a big company. He had stopped the car smack in the middle of a badly-lit street late at night, without warning, and got out to pee. Returning to the vehicle, he told her to get out since he had to urgently go elsewhere. Rather than give in to the fear she felt, Ritu had asked him where he hailed from, and on learning it was from the Dharwad region, she had switched to the dialect of Kannada they spoke there and started berating him, asking him how he would like it if his mother or sister were in the position she was in now.

'And that worked?' asked a less-than-impressed Aditi when Ritu had told her about the incident. 'I think that was stupid, Ritu. What if he had turned violent?'

'It was in the middle of nowhere! I just couldn't have got down there. I took a calculated risk but it worked. He subsided sulkily, told me it had been a bad week for him, that the aggregators weren't paying him on time and other such sob stories, all the way till we reached here. I promised not to report him. We almost became close pals.'

Now Aditi watched Aditya press a finger to the bridge of his nose.

'You look tired,' she told him softly.

'I'm okay,' he replied. 'Let's go home. I need to hold you close.'

A thought suddenly struck Aditi.

'We can't go home, unless we want to join the party,' she told him.

'What party?' Aditya threw her an enquiring look.

'Ritu's having some of her work colleagues over this evening. I made humungous heaps of khow suey for them.'

He grinned appreciatively. 'No, I meant, let's go to my place. You haven't seen it yet, have you?'

Biting back a retort, Aditi shook her head. She hadn't seen it yet only because he had not asked her over yet. Her boyfriend was not one who rushed into anything. They had been dating for over six months now and this was the first time he'd invited her home.

She knew he lived on Berlie Street, in a quiet part of what was now a not-very-quiet city. They turned into an apartment complex that looked very elegant but not very new. The security guard threw him a smiling salute as Aditya glided to a stop in a parking bay. There was already a car there, a gleam of blueish silver. A Merc convertible.

'Yours?' she asked Aditya, who threw the car an affectionate look and nodded a yes.

'Well!' exclaimed Aditi. 'If you brought the car instead of your bike on our dates, I could have worn my…'

'Aditi Pillai, I love those flowing skirts of yours,' Aditya said laughing. 'But if you wore them all the time, I'd miss out on seeing those legs. And with legs like yours, that would be a real crime.' He grinned and she tossed her curls disdainfully, though pleased at his compliment. She was in a dress that clung lovingly to her curves tonight; it was a brand-new buy and Aditi had been dying to wear it. It had taken some adroit manipulation to get on the bike, but was well worth it just to see that look in his eyes every time he glanced at her.

His apartment on the tenth floor was rather like his car, more in the classical mould than anything too trendy. Someone—his mother? Sister-in-law? An interior decorator?—had done up the place in muted earth shades. Olive green cushions on a beige sofa, thick silken ochre-coloured drapes, a rug that lightened things up while reflecting the shades of the room. It was all minimal chic till you looked at the walls. While an extra-large television took up most of one wall, the standout piece that covered a lot of the facing wall was a giant triptych of abstract art. Scarlets, blacks, navy, azure, emerald, gold all flowed together in a strangely harmonious and cohesive pattern.

She threw him an enquiring look. He named one of Bangalore's popular young artists, adding casually 'He's a good friend. This was before he took up art photography as a full-time profession.'

'What will you have to drink, Aditi?' he then asked, walking over to a walnut-wood bar that stood in one corner of the dining section.

He hadn't asked but Aditi said, 'I like your apartment.'

At which, he looked up at her and smiled a toe-curling smile.

'I'm glad you do,' he said. There was a moment of silence while they looked at each other intensely.

Then the spell broke and she said, 'I'll have some white wine, please. Are we ordering in for dinner?'

'We could if that's what you want,' he replied. 'But I think Radhamma will have cooked dinner and left it in the kitchen.'

Aditi followed him into the large kitchen, feeling her heart leap with delight at the visual treat it presented. The wall in there was clad with exposed brick, there was an island counter in the middle of the room and on it, she could see covered dishes neatly laid out.

'Who is Radhamma?' she asked.

'Well, her name is Radha, and I affix "amma" to it, so Radhamma. She is the family cook. Once I moved in here, I asked if she would come in a few days a week and cook for me, and she was more than happy to.'

Radhamma had indeed cooked up a storm for Aditya. Lifting the lids off the various casseroles, they discovered a dal, two veggies, a meat and spinach dish, fluffy white rice and a mound of soft rotis carefully wrapped in a cloth napkin.

'Aditya!' Aditi exclaimed.

He was sniffing the food appreciatively. 'What?' he asked, looking up at her.

'Your Radhamma cooks food like this every time she comes here?'

'Well, yes,' he said.

'And then what happens to all the food on the days you eat out? Or do you eat at home most nights?'

'Most nights we don't meet, you mean? Yes, I eat at home usually. And she cooks only when I tell her I'll be home to eat her food.'

He smoothly moved over to where she was standing and looped his arms around her from behind, bending his head to nuzzle the nape of her neck.

'I told her I'd be bringing a friend home for dinner tonight,' he told her.

'Smooth operator,' she chuckled but Aditya wasn't listening. He was busy trailing a series of small kisses along her neck. She shivered in delight.

He lifted his dark head and shot her a suggestive smile. 'Mmmm' he told her in agreement, before spinning her around and bending his head to kiss her. Aditi kissed him back whole-heartedly.

When he lifted his head, she reached up on her toes to trail kisses on his jawline, feeling a pulse come to life, then race, under her lips.

'Aditi, Aditi,' he said softly, running his open palm up and down her jersey silk dress. The zig-zag printed fabric lifted where he applied pressure to it, stayed ruched for a moment, and then fell back to hug her curves lovingly. Aditya cupped her bottom over the dress, making his move slowly so she had time to pull back if she wanted.

But Aditi wanted nothing of the sort. It was about time, she thought languorously. Curving her slender arms about his neck, she pulled him closer for another kiss. This time, during the kiss, one of his hands moved between their bodies, came up to cup a breast. She sighed into his mouth. It felt so good.

The next kiss went up several notches and caught fire. Aditya picked her up and carried her over to the couch and gently laid her down there, his eyes sending a clear message of intent to her. She smiled back, her eyes said this was what she wanted, and he came down lightly beside her on his side, smiling down at her.

'Aditi,' he said.

'What?' she asked looking at him through half-closed eyes. She was feeling shy suddenly and rather unexpectedly, wondering if she could ask him to lower the lights in the room. For all the cool vibes Aditi Pillai gave out, her close friends knew what Aditya didn't: she dated casually, she did not really do serious relationships. This now was beginning to take on a serious air.

'Nothing,' he said. 'Just Aditi.' And in one fluid motion, he pulled her gently upright while pulling the dress over her head. Aditi mentally sent up thanks that the fit and texture of her dress had demanded a gossamer bra and a pair of thongs. He caught his breath looking at her skin gleaming against the soft green of her bra and panties.

'You are gorgeous,' he told her huskily, seriously, as he bent to kiss her throat.

Suddenly so nervous her teeth were almost chattering, Aditi found herself saying, 'Thank you' even as the humour in the situation hit her. Get your mojo back, girl, she told herself silently, and then recovered her poise. Almost of its own volition, her hands went to his shirt-front and she slipped the buttons free, one by one. He sat up and shucked the shirt off, exposing a toned torso.

Aditi ran one hand over his taut stomach and asked him in all seriousness, 'You work out a lot, huh?'

He raised an eyebrow, even as his mouth stretched into a wide smile.

'Funny girl,' he told her lovingly. Then he bent purposefully to her.

When the doorbell went, both of them did not hear it at first. But whoever was at the door had their finger pressed firmly on the buzzer. Aditya sat up suddenly and ran a hand through his rumpled hair.

She shot him an enquiring look. He shrugged in reply. They hastily got back into their clothes, feeling their heartbeats settle to a normal pace.

It was a somewhat composed Aditya who opened the door while Aditi sat in as demure a fashion as she could on the sofa. Only the heightened colour in their cheeks was a dead give-away, if one was looking.

The woman who came in almost rushing into the room was not looking. She was in one word, stunning. She had a long lean face with a model-like bone structure and lovely dark eyes which now held a very worried look in them. She was slight of frame but it was her hair that was striking. Obviously very long, it was caught up in a heavy bun at the nape of a delicate neck and it was evenly layered with black and white strands. The salt-and-pepper hair was a striking contrast to the young face. She was a real beauty and Aditi found herself staring.

The woman ignored her though, she had eyes only for Aditya. 'Adit,' she burst out. 'Come home quickly. It's…' then her eyes moved to Aditi and she cut her words off, a strange look coming into her eyes. Was it hostility? Aditi couldn't quite make out.

Whoa, she thought, a bit startled, and wishing she was anywhere but here at this point in time.

But Aditya had the situation in hand. Lightly pressing the woman's slender shoulder, he went into the kitchen and emerged with a glass of water in his hand. She took it with a shaking hand and drank it down, splashing quite a bit on herself in the process.

He bent his head close to hers and murmured something. She nodded in reply. Aditi looked away.

'Aditi,' he said and she looked at him. 'This is Preetha. Preetha, meet my girlfriend Aditi.'

Now Preetha looked distinctly startled, so startled that Aditi knew this was a first, meeting one of his girlfriends. As distractions went, it was an effective one because she seemed to collect herself, then offered Aditi a wan smile and apologized for barging in like this.

'That's okay, you didn't interrupt anything,' Aditya told her while Aditi avoided looking at him and smiled hesitantly at the woman. Was Preetha the sister-in-law he had mentioned in passing? They had established that Aditi was his girlfriend but there was no word on who the other woman was.

A bit annoyed now, Aditi stared hard at him but was met with an opaque look. She knew him well enough by now to understand his mind was elsewhere, racing, probably addressing whatever dilemma Preetha had come to him with. It was clear the woman was battling with some problem.

All three of them stood frozen in an awkward tableau, the women just standing around waiting for the man to do something, to say something. The air was thrumming with an undefined tension but Aditi just couldn't put her finger on what it was.

Aditya spoke. 'Give me a moment, Preetha,' he instructed (His wife? Sister? Cousin? Housekeeper, Aditi wondered wildly). 'We'll drop Aditi off, then...'

She cut in firmly. 'No need for that, Aditya. I'll call myself a cab.'

His brow cleared and he said, 'Are you sure?' At her nod, he then said, 'Okay. I'll call for one of our cabs. Thanks, Aditi.'

And as the three of them moved out of his apartment five minutes later, Aditya's protective arm across Preetha's delicate shoulders, the latter turned to Aditi inside the lift and said, on the ghost of an amused laugh, 'Aditi. And Aditya. Look at that. Your names match.'

CHAPTER FIVE

'And that was that?' asked a somewhat mystified Mickey. They were sitting at Bangalore's most popular sushi bar which had a skyline view so glitzy, Mickey said it almost made you forget the roads choked with traffic far down below. Aditi couldn't disagree. They had just wound up a client meeting, the client showing excellent taste in asking to meet here, and were now relaxing with celebratory drinks.

'That was three weeks ago and yes, that was that,' admitted a slightly despondent Aditi.

Mickey ran a concerned eye over her. She made a pretty picture, gleaming curls cascading gloriously onto bare shoulders, her golden tube top matching the butis on her navy skirt. But he knew her well enough and there was no missing the slight sadness in her eyes.

'Fuck,' he ground out now, in irritation. That shook her out of her reverie and she chuckled throatily. 'Language, language. What would Minu say?'

Minu was Mickey's wife of just a year, a sweet-faced girl whose unsophisticated good nature was both a byword and a relief to Mickey's friends. They'd been more than a bit aghast when he had gone off to Kapurthala to marry a Punjabi girl chosen for him by his bua. Of course Pia, Raman, Aditi had all gone along as part of the baraat and danced with abandon at his shaadi. Luckily, this arranged match had worked very well and now the Snack Team often plonked themselves down at Mickey's pad, demanding home-cooked food from a willing Minu whose cooking was, according to them, totes Cordon Bleu level.

'No, seriously,' said Mickey, bringing the focus of the conversation back to her. 'They left, you left and since then not a word?'

'Not a word,' she said dolefully. 'Maybe he's gone out of town. Maybe he's super busy.'

'Maybe he's a bloody...' bit out Mickey. 'Aditi, how long have you been seeing this bloke now?'

Aditi thought for a moment. 'Some seven months,' she told him.

'Well, that's not a very short time. I'm not saying he ought to have proposed to you after six-seven months of dating. But you guys have been seeing each other exclusively and ought to know all about one another. You ought to at least know if there's a Preetha in his life and who Preetha is. He's such a damned close-mouthed fellow. Doesn't even mix much with us, does he?' The last line was thrown at her with ill-concealed belligerence.

Aditi sighed. That was true. She had tried on quite a few occasions to get them all together, to go watch a movie, go pub-crawling, partying, but Aditya invariably found some excuse to cry off. He was polite, as chatty as a quiet man like him could manage, quite friendly when he ran into her friends. But that was it. There didn't seem to be any desire on his part to deepen his friendship with the few people who mattered so much to Aditi.

Now Mickey was all riled up. 'Maybe he thinks he's better than us,' he scowled fiercely, alarming a passing waiter.

At that, Aditi had to protest. Whatever else Aditya Shenoy was, he was no snob. He was just a careful, cautious man, economical with his words and actions and apparently with his emotions, too.

'You know something, you can do better,' Mickey said now and before she could help it, Aditi cried out, 'No!'

Something in her voice stopped her friend in his tracks, stopped him cold. He stared at her in dismay. 'Addy?' he asked. 'You don't do serious, remember?'

Oh, what the hell, thought Aditi. *I walked into that one, didn't I?* She said on a wistful sigh, 'I know I don't, Micks. And I'm not saying I'm looking for more than what Aditya and I have going at this point. But benching me like this? Bloody hell, no one does that to me!'

'No one benches Baby?' Mickey burst out laughing, just as she had intended. How could she possibly tell him that though she—famously—didn't do serious, Aditya Shenoy now possessed pretty much all her waking thoughts, that she sat at client meetings doodling his name and doing elaborate calligraphy with floral motifs around that name? That his smiling eyes, well-defined jawline, the shape of his fingers and his mouth had begun appearing in her dreams, too?

Aditi Pillai had caught it and caught it bad. Thankfully, Mickey didn't see, or if he did, he didn't comment on it. 'Ah, let's do some shots,' he said. 'Just what we both need.'

'Just what *you* need?' she said, making an effort to rallying round. 'What's your problem?'

'Minu's off to Kapurthala next week. For a whole month.'

Chuckling, they took themselves to the bar where they proceeded to down shots, making enough of a ruckus to have several laughing glances thrown their way.

'Okay,' announced Mickey after a while. 'Last round. Let's dedicate it to…cads?'

She cracked up at that. Cads? Who but Mickey used words like that?

'Cads, it shall be,' she declared, lifting her glass and throwing it down with a graceful gesture. Putting down the glass, she looked up and there was Cad Number One standing at her side. Was she hallucinating?

'Cad?' she found herself asking him. Something sparked in his eyes and it was not amusement. She stared mesmerized. Mickey cackled, then caught sight of Aditya and his laughter petered out into silence.

'Hi, Aditi,' Aditya said softly.

'I'm not alone,' she told him caustically. 'You know Mickey, don't you?'

He turned slowly to the other man, smiled politely, all urbane polish. 'Hey man, long time no see.'

'Yes, and you'll keep it that way if you can help it, right?' Mickey asked challengingly. Aditya raised a cool eyebrow and stared consideringly at Mickey.

Aditi, meanwhile, was devouring him with her eyes. It had been a long three weeks and only the best kind of self-control had stopped her from reaching for the phone or taking a leaf out of his book and texting him continuously, as he had done long before. Actually, she *had* sent him one message. It had received no response and her self-esteem had quickly reasserted itself, thankfully. She had felt bad but not really devastated. Something told her that Aditya would get back in touch when he wanted to, not before, and she didn't want to make an ass of herself, coming over all despo. It was just that she really, really missed him, dayyumm.

He looked gorgeous but just a little tired. He was in formal attire, a tie of emerald silk neatly knotted in place, making his cream-coloured shirt gleam. This was the first time she'd seen him so formally dressed and she swallowed; formal really suited him.

Aditya shot Mickey an even look and said, 'Why would I want to avoid you? I've just been busy. Very busy.'

The two men's eyes locked and held for an interminably long time, then Mickey dropped his gaze. Mickey was a good friend to Aditi. He wasn't going to rub the other man up the wrong way, not if Aditya was dating Aditi right now.

Aditya turned to Aditi. 'How have you been?' he asked in a low voice that seemed to actually caress her skin. But it was time to make him sweat a bit, she decided.

'I'm okay,' she replied shortly. 'How have you been? And Preetha?'

He opened his mouth to say something, then obviously thought the better of it and kept quiet. That was typical of Aditya. Then, he bent down and kissed the corner of her mouth. That was *not* typical of Aditya. The action caught her by surprise and she recoiled in surprise. His hand shot out, held her gently but firmly in place for a few seconds.

After which, he straightened up, sent Mickey a speaking look and told Aditi, 'I'll call you. Later tonight. Bye, love.'

Outside, they called a cab but not a Caboyea car. As she got in, she turned a gleeful face to her friend. 'He called me love,' she breathed.

Mickey's usual good humour asserted itself. 'Okay, I'll remember that,' he assured her. Then a puzzled look came over his face. 'Am I to remember that?' he asked, sounding rather confused. 'Why am I to remember that?'

~

Aditi was fatigued by the time Mickey dropped her off at her place. All the liquor-induced euphoria had worn off and reality had sunk in: she had a boyfriend who took her for granted. He called her when he felt like it, neglected her at other times. He was close-mouthed, secretive.

He deserved to be dumped. *And I would dump him too, if I didn't like him so much, if I wasn't having so much fun with him,* she thought, a little angry at both Aditya and herself.

She let herself into the apartment, hoping against hope Ritu wouldn't be in. She really didn't feel like chatting tonight.

But it was not her night and Ritu emerged from the kitchen area, cradling a giant mug of something steaming hot. 'I heated up some of your cauliflower soup,' she told Aditi, then asked, 'How did the client meeting go?'

Aditi racked her brains, trying to remember what seemed to have happened a decade ago. 'It went well,' she replied, not trying to disguise her mood or her tiredness.

The next thing she knew, she was being hustled into her bedroom and into her bed.

'I have to brush my teeth and change,' protested Aditi.

'Do that later, chill a bit now. You look dog-tired. Was the pitch that tough?'

Aditi began to laugh helplessly. 'No, the pitch went like a dream, they were quite taken with the idea of mini pizza wedges with all the toppings we suggested, though they did say they wanted more veggie toppings than meat ones.'

Ritu was perched on Aditi's rocking chair, trying not to rock back and forth because that bugged Aditi, and also because she was trying to drink her soup. She proffered the mug to Aditi, who shook her head.

'Have you eaten?' asked the perceptive Ritu. 'You are so crabby when you are famished. It's the...'

'...hangry syndrome. I know. You point it out often enough.' Aditi frowned at her, then relented and said, 'No, I haven't had dinner. Minu had kept food for both of us at their place but I wasn't hungry.'

'What?' asked Ritu then, so loudly that Aditi looked up, startled.

'What?' she asked again. 'What?'

'Now you are sounding like the chorus from a musical,' Aditi said, cracking a faint smile. Ritu continued to regard her under furrowed brows. 'What happened?' she asked in a stern tone and Aditi laughed helplessly.

'Oh, I ran into Aditya Shenoy at the restaurant.'

'And?' prompted Ritu.

'And nothing. Mickey was nasty to him, I was nasty to him.' Aditi brightened at the recollection.

'Was he crushed?' asked a distinctly sceptical Ritu.

'No, not in the least,' admitted Aditi. 'In fact, he kissed me in front of Micks.'

'He did? Wow! How territorial!' Ritu exclaimed, laughing.

'Well, it was a side-of-the-mouth kiss,' Aditi felt impelled to say. 'But it was strange, PDA from such a reticent man.'

'He'd been out of town?' Ritu asked and Aditi realized that her friend and flatmate was well aware that Aditya had not been in touch with her.

'I don't know,' she burst out. 'I don't think so. I don't care.'

'Good,' nodded Ritu, keeping an impassive face. 'Decided to move on?'

'No!' exclaimed Aditi then, 'Oh, go away,' she told Ritu crossly.

'I will, in a bit,' the other girl said. 'I just want to ask you one question, Addy.'

'What?' Aditi growled.

'What do you know about Aditya Shenoy? How well do you think you know him?' demanded Ritu.

Aditi looked at Ritu through a curtain of curls. 'What are you implying? Is he the Bangalore Brute?'

'Er, who is the Bangalore Brute?' Ritu looked staggered, and Aditi limpidly said, 'I dunno. I just made him up.' Both the girls fell about laughing. They laughed so hard, Ritu's soup sloshed onto the dhurrie below and Aditi's hair broke free of its restraining scrunchie and fell gloriously all about her face. Her mood immediately rose. Nothing could be so bad if they could laugh like this, nothing. Not an annoying boyfriend, at least.

When they sobered up and were smiling foolishly at each other, Ritu said simply, 'I Googled Aditya. Have you?'

'Would you believe it, no,' replied Aditi slowly. She couldn't believe Ritu had done such a thing. Ritu was over the Miss Malati act and now got on well with Aditya. She had a fondness for stand-up comedy and EDM which Aditya ragged her mercilessly about, and having found he had briefly been a fan of ghazals a long time ago, she gave as good as she got, launching into a soulful ghazal every time he came home. They were good friends now. Or so Aditi thought. And of course she had not Googled her close-mouthed boyfriend, though now that she thought about it, it was more due to lack of time than lack of intent. But she didn't tell Ritu that.

'It says,' said Ritu, ticking each bullet point dramatically off her fingers. 'That he's moderately wealthy, by himself. That he may have over-reached with his business venture, Caboyea, since he has taken some heavy loans to get the concern up and running. That Caboyea is doing well but still in tightrope-walk mode. That he is reclusive, doesn't attend Page Three parties.' Aditi snorted at this point. She knew well enough that he was not the most outgoing of men, not that she seriously minded.

Ritu was not yet finished. 'He is crazy about bikes. Owns a whole garage of them: Harley, Ducati, Enfield, Yamaha, vintage and souped-up models.'

But Aditi was thinking of something other than her boyfriend's supposed obsession with bikes. 'You said he was moderately rich, by himself. What *does* that mean?'

Ritu looked at her. 'I was coming to that. Aditya is Sudarshan Kamath's son.' She sat back, satisfied by the bombshell she had just dropped.

Aditi stared at her friend, astonished. Sudarshan Kamath's son? Sudarshan Kamath was the city's most notorious liquor baron, the man with fingers in as many business pies as possible, industries that spanned aviation, hotels, a floating casino in a neighbouring state. He had even sponsored the country's premier beauty contest for many years running; then the maverick tycoon had become bored and abruptly dropped the sponsorship.

'You know something,' Ritu said almost chattily, 'he does resemble Sudarshan Kamath. Same fair skin, slim build, aquiline nose.'

'Who is his mother?' Aditi asked huskily.

'His mother is Kamath's first wife.'

Now she had Aditi's full attention again. The wheels in her head were slowly turning. 'Raj and Aditya's mother is Kamath's first wife,' she enunciated slowly.

'Shakunthala, that's the first wife's name,' nodded Ritu. 'Sudarshan Kamath had two sons with her.'

She continued, 'Shakunthala and Sudarshan Kamath divorced many years ago. Then he married a socialite, Shehnaz Something. A Parsi. No kids.'

Looking suitably gratified that her news report had been a total scoop, Ritu continued. 'And wait for this. A few years ago, Shehnaz dumped Sudarshan Kamath for some Argentinian cattle baron! Close your mouth,' she kindly advised Aditi.

But the cattle baron detail had set both girls off again. They laughed till their sides hurt. 'C...c...c...cattle baron,' choked Aditi. 'Poor Aditya...!'

'Poor Aditya? You mean poor Sudarshan Kamath! He was the one who got dumped for...what do you call an Argentinian rancher? Hombre? Capitano? Whatever.'

'No, I *don't* mean poor Sudarshan Kamath,' retorted Aditi. 'From what I see and hear, the man has got over his wife's desertion with remarkable alacrity. He's dating that film star about three decades younger than him, isn't he?'

Then she looked up. 'Why doesn't Aditya use his father's last name? Why isn't he Aditya Kamath?' She shot the question in an almost accusing fashion at her friend.

Now Ritu looked as mystified as she sounded. 'That, Google doesn't tell us. Probably Kamath's first wife and her sons don't wish to have anything to do with the man?' On cue, Aditi's phone pinged.

Long day and it didn't go too well either the message read.

'Aditya Whatsisname?' asked Ritu.

'Hmmm,' said Aditi, looking at the next message. **Just can't summon up the energy to call tonight. But. We need to talk.** Her lips twisted in a sarcastic grimace at that. A concerned Ritu said, 'Hey! What's up?'

'Aditya says we need to talk.'

'Wowie!' Ritu sounded impressed. 'I mean, how many men say that, huh?'

'Idiot,' Aditi said without heat, then thought for a long moment and added, 'Actually, no man I know. And I'm going to sleep now.'

Ritu paused at the doorway, mug of now cold soup in hand, her hair a thick swathe on her shoulder and down her back.

'You okay, na?' she asked, trying to sound as offhand as she could.

And Aditi was able to assure her with perfect sincerity, 'Yes. I'm good. I'll be better after a good night's sleep.'

This was true, too. She was quite shocked about the Aditya-Sudarshan Kamath reveal but she was also sure her boyfriend would have got around to telling her, in his own fashion, in his own time. That was the way the rather secretive Aditya Shenoy worked. His family history probably played a huge part in shaping his personality; all this wives-kids-surnames jumble was making *her* head spin. Poor Aditya had to live with it, live in it.

But she would make things better for Aditya. Because she suddenly recognized her role. She was going to be a one-woman squad that comprised Aditya Shenoy's well-being and protection squad. His wingwoman.

After she had dutifully brushed her teeth, washed the make-up off her face and got into a demure eyelet embroidered nightgown, Aditi went along the corridor and knocked on Ritu's door. Entering the room, she announced, 'I know something Google doesn't about Aditya Shenoy.'

Ritu's eyes gleamed. 'Tell, tell,' she urged. 'The colour of his shorts?'

'Yikes!' Aditi said. 'Why would I tell you that? I know...' and here she paused dramatically. 'That he absolutely adores Batman. He has an amazing collection of Batman comics.'

Ritu immediately came back to this with, 'And does he go for all the Comic Cons in costume?' To which Aditi said something very rude and her friend cackled and made to throw a pillow at her. Aditi exited hastily, went back to her room and got into bed. She hadn't responded to his messages but that hadn't bothered him because he'd signed off anyway. *Too cool a cucumber, dude*, she muttered. *That's gotta change.*

Almost on cue, Aditi's boring-as-hell good angel woke up after a hiatus. *He's just your boyfriend,* the creature protested. *He doesn't need you to try and change him. Or come all protective over him.*

He does too, retorted Aditi spiritedly.

No. He's a grown man and you keep telling yourself you are not serious about him.

What does being serious have to do with anything, Aditi asked her good angel. *I'm here to bring sunshine and radiance into his life. And I intend to do just that, so there.*

That pretty much shut the angel up, she noticed with satisfaction.

~

The next morning, before setting out to work, an uncharacteristically serious Ritu told Aditi, 'Do me one favour. One big favour. Do NOT bring up the topic of Sudarshan Kamath with Aditya Shenoy until he tells you about it on his own. Please?'

'I wasn't going to,' Aditi replied a tad sulkily. She got an exasperated look for her pains.

'Yeah, right. Remember, I know you. You blab the first thing in your head and all consequences be damned. Not this time, please Addy.'

'Why?' she asked Ritu, curious inspite of herself.

'Because unlike some of the randos you have dated previously, this is a sweet guy. Only he's got issues, seemingly major ones. Don't scare him away. Let him unburden himself to you in his own time. Deal?'

Nodding in agreement, Aditi nonetheless felt impelled to protest, 'I didn't date randos. I don't date randos.'

'Don't get me started,' her friend replied acidly but picked up her bright pink jhola and went off to work.

The first thing Mickey told her in the office when they sat down to iron out the fine details of the mini pizzas project was, 'Did you know your Aditya is the son of…of all people…Sudarshan Kamath?'

Aditi gaped at him. 'You know about his father?' she asked.

'Well, I Googled the fellow last night.'

'You did?' gasped Aditi

'Yes, why are you acting so weird? Not a crime to Google people, the last time I checked.'

'No well, only because it was Google-Aditya-Shenoy night, last night,' she told Mickey, a grin on her face.

Mickey let out a loud bark of amusement, leading Raman in the far corner of the room to shush him.

'You too?'

She shook her head.

'Ah, Ritu,' he said.

'Mmm.'

'Okay but listen up, Addy. Don't go asking him all about that father of his, okay? It's rough on the fellow, having such a flamboyant father. Let's give him a break…'

'Let *us*? Where do you barge in between my boyfriend and me?' she asked, shooting one eyebrow up expressively and he chuckled.

'I mean, *you* give him a break.'

'I will,' she promised Mickey and she meant it.

But she didn't get to meet Aditya all that week. The pizza project was a big one, only the client was rather eccentric and contacted them almost daily with a range of bizarre ideas regarding the snacks he wanted. The Snack Team was dealing with it directly only because the excellent kitchen people contracted for the venture were a bit handicapped by their lack of communication skills. The client wanted never-before-used veggies on the pizza wedges and it was tough telling him baingan and avarakkai were not going to add much to the flavour at all.

On his part, Caboyea was pitching for a big Canadian partner. Aditya told her as much, skimming over the finer details. They had got back to speaking to each other every night, and to all intents and purposes it was as if the strain of the inexplicable silence over the last three weeks had done a fade-out.

Aditi had no intention of letting him off the hook so easily regarding that long silence but the issue was not going to be resolved over the phone, so she decided to shut up and put up for the time being.

Not that she had to put up with much, because Aditya, surprise, surprise, turned out to be amazingly adept at mobile courting. Over the phone, her boyfriend shed his innate reticence and became one liquid-tongued lover, murmuring stuff into her ear in a low, husky voice, stuff that had her all het up and excited at times, laughing at other times, and at still other times, sighing in a gooey fashion. Even though she refused to acknowledge it to herself, this Aditya dude was making her fall deeper in love with him.

Does he tell you he loves you, asked that sceptical voice of her evil angel from inside her head.

No.

But have you told him you love him?

No was the answer there too.

So, it's quits, Aditi decided sleepily, plumping up a pillow and closing her eyes.

CHAPTER SIX

As things turned out, when she next met Aditya Shenoy, it wasn't on a pre-arranged date. The Snack Team had made all the necessary arrangements for the short eats to be served at a private party at Bangalore's numero uno club, and she had been deputed to go with Raman and check things out.

'What does that mean?' she asked, tucking her curls into a topknot and securing it with a ballpen. 'That I go eat dinner with the Lancasters and the Yorks?'

Raman and Mickey burst into laughter even as Pia, on cue, wrinkled her fair brow and asked, 'Are they doing a *GoT* shoot at the Club then?"

The news was gently broken to both that no, there was no shoot at the club and to Aditi that no, she wasn't actually invited to the do, she just needed to drop by the kitchens and see how it all was going, along with the food man in their team, Raman.

Pia's brow remained wrinkled, but with good reason this time. 'Why?' she asked, 'It's not catering we are doing, is it? We've done our bit, got the two concerned parties together, now they should take it forward.'

She had a point. Aditi cocked an eyebrow at Mickey. There was a moment's silence during which no one missed the admiring look Raman threw at Pia, no one but Pia that is. Then Mickey said slowly, 'The thing is…' and Aditi knew. If this went well, something big was coming the Snack Team's way next.

'Okay, okay' she said in a mock-aggressive tone. 'But I'm not dressing up to go stand in the kitchens of the Club.'

And she didn't dress up, either. Only to run smack into Aditya and an older man as she came out of the kitchen area into the large corridor. The porch lighting there was always borderline Twilight Zone and Aditi found herself peering short-sightedly at them.

'Hi, Aditi,' her boyfriend said softly.

Suddenly Aditi felt breathless. OMG, she thought, he looked dishy as hell. He was wearing a dark suit with an amethyst-coloured tie and was totally killing it. All she could do was stare foolishly at him, pulse racing and heart thudding. If she had her way, she'd keep him in suits, they suited him so well!

Talk, Aditi, she told herself desperately, and managed to squeak out an 'Oh, hi.'

The man beside Aditya gave a sharp crack of laughter. 'Aditya meets Aditi? Now, that's cute!'

Aditi glared at him, about to roll her eyes dramatically, then hastily converted the look into one of impassive blankness when she recognized Sudarshan Kamath. This was Aditya's father. He was here with his father. So obviously they got on.

Having given in to curiosity at last, and because she'd rather she did it herself than have her friends do it for her, she had searched for Aditya online. She had pored over snaps of his father and him, seeking a resemblance but not finding much of one. Standing side by side though, there was more than a fleeting resemblance between the two men, in the sharp line of jaw, the cleft in the chin and the way both fixed you with a direct gaze from piercing dark eyes.

Now Aditya said smoothly, 'Oh, it gets cuter. She's my girlfriend. Aditi, this is my father.' The way he made the introduction, it was clear he expected Aditi to know the man and the fact that the man was his father.

Sudarshan Kamath came up closer, apparently all the better to subject Aditi to a quick scrutiny, no less intense for its fleeting duration. For the first time in her young life, Aditi felt underdressed. The skirt she was wearing tonight was a deep pink one paired with a simple sleeveless indigo top, cut away to reveal the fine bones of her shoulders as well as her collarbone. Her rust-toned chunni was serving as a stole and was draped in casual fashion about her shoulders.

Eeep, she thought before her pragmatism reasserted itself: she was not on show for Mr Moneybags Kamath. She was here on work and this was attire suited to that purpose. Mr Kamath— and Mr Shenoy, for that matter—could put that in their pipes and smoke it.

She looked across at Aditya and watched his eyes crinkling with amusement as he caught the faintly prickly waves that rose off her. He slowly, deliberately, looked her over, from her jutti-clad feet to the top of her glossy curls and then he looked into her eyes, naked desire in his. They locked glances for a long minute, then she looked back at Sudarshan Kamath, her breathing a little uneven.

Sudarshan Kamath was soon shooting the breeze with her and Aditi understood just how this man had come by his reputation of being a lady-killer. He had a way of looking deep into your eyes, inclining himself slightly towards you, as if to absorb all the nuggets of wisdom you were going to let fall from your lips. Even at such close quarters, the man gave a good physical account of himself, his body as firm and supple as that of a younger man, quite belying his age, which Aditi knew to be over sixty, the thick salt-and-pepper hair styled elegantly above a very distinguished face, the ineffable air of power he gave off, all of it quite impressive.

Now the older man turned to his son who stood silently, watchfully beside him. 'She's a terrific gal,' he announced. Terrific! Aditi's nose wrinkled just a little and as her eyes met Aditya's, they shared a moment of pure amusement.

'Will I meet you again?' Sudarshan Kamath asked her.

'I don't know,' Aditi shot back smiling sweetly at him. 'Will you?'

She had somehow expected to take an immediate dislike for whatever reason, when she met Aditya's father now that she knew who he was, but she found she quite liked the man. Was it right to warm to her boyfriend's estranged father? But were they estranged? Aditya did not carry the Kamath surname but then again, he had introduced her to his father smoothly, without any hesitation. Just what *was* their relationship? More mystery, dash it! It was a good thing Aditi didn't do proprietial much.

'Came to meet someone?' Aditya asked her now and she told him briskly just what she was doing there. 'I think you'll like the aperitifs,' she dimpled at him. 'I'm sure I will,' he said smoothly, his face bland and polite. *Pompous ass*, she thought. *Was he behaving like this because his father was around?*

Sudarshan Kamath lifted a hand in farewell and walked on.

'Took a cab here?' Aditya asked her and she dragged her gaze away from the retreating figure of his father and fixed it back on him.

'No, Raman and I came together but he's still in the kitchens. I'm off to the nearest Metro station,' she said, shaking her head, the curls bouncing off her shoulders like they had a life of their own. Now it was his turn to stare riveted at her hair till Aditi felt self-conscious and asked him testily, 'What?'

'Nothing,' he said. 'I'll get you dropped home, shall I? I'm sorry but I'm expected inside so I can't take you home myself.'

Suddenly, she felt a jolt of mischief run through her.

'Would you?' she asked, adopting a coquettish tone, and his breath caught.

'Would I what?' he asked her huskily but his eyes told her he knew just what she was talking about.

'Would you like to take me home yourself?'

Something molten stirred in those deep eyes. 'Yes,' he told her, lowering his voice to an intimate drawl. 'I'd like, no, I'd love to take you home. To my home.'

'And then?' she asked, her be-ringed fingers playing with the spiral strands that fell from her shoulder.

'And then, we could do stuff. A lot of interesting stuff,' Aditya Shenoy smiled meaningfully at her. It was obvious he was enjoying this.

She fixed him with a direct gaze then broke the spell calmly and deliberately.

'Alright,' she told him cheerily. 'Just wanted to know. And yes, thanks, I'd love to get a drop home.'

He laughed softly, then asked her, 'When are you going to get yourself a car?' This was his constant refrain, ever since he'd found out that she could drive expertly, as expertly as she could ride his Ducati. No amount of telling him that she didn't enjoy driving in Bangalore's endless bottlenecked traffic, on the city's bad roads, seemed to quite convince him that she was better off riding in the Metro and in cabs. Now when he riffed on that old tune again, she simply shot him a dark look and refused to reply. He chuckled, not in the least put out.

He walked her the short distance to the car park, speaking softly into his phone. And then the vehicle that was to drop her home came gliding up rather like James Bond's Aston Martin and Aditi forgot all about her reticent boyfriend for the moment.

It was a gleam of the deepest green, a Lamborghini Huracan. To complete the picture, a uniformed driver sat at the wheel, his peaked cap perched jauntily on his head. Aditi turned to her boyfriend with an exaggerated mouth-drop and he laughed. Not for a moment did she miss the unamused ring in that laugh. 'It's my father's car. I'm sure every Bangalorean who reads Page Three knows of my father's er, flashy lifestyle.'

Aditi knew better than to let this get too deep, so she laughed, batted her eyelids at him and said, 'Oh, this is amaze. I'm all for the flashy life if it means a ride in a Lamborghini.'

He started to say quietly, 'But I don't have one,' then looked into her eyes and caught the gentle mockery there.

'Yes, I know,' she forestalled him. 'You drive a cab. But you can always borrow your father's car to give Caboyea's loyal customers a luxury ride. Think about it.'

Aditya visibly relaxed, then smiled. It was such a devastating smile, Aditi threw whatever little caution she had to the winds and stepped closer to him. 'Kiss me,' she ordered him softly.

He didn't bat an eyelid. He didn't cast a quick look around, though she knew there was no one around. He didn't look at the driver who was staring fixedly ahead, windows rolled up. He didn't ask 'Here and now?'

Instead, he caught her up in an embrace that was both fluid yet firm and bent his head to hers. Aditi closed her eyes blissfully, then lifted a hand to caress that lean jaw. They kissed as if their lives depended on it, which perhaps it did, then broke free, both of them breathing heavily.

Aditi then slid gracefully into the sleek confines of the beige leather interior of the car, like she'd been getting in and out of Lamborghinis all her life. She arranged her skirt about her and lifted a hand in farewell with all the panache of a Sudarshan Kamath, as the bottle-green car glided smoothly away. And for the first time in all her Bangalore days, Aditi didn't curse the usual chock-a-block traffic on the roads. She also adopted bottle-green as her favourite colour du jour.

She quickly phoned Ritu to come sauntering out casually to get an eyeful of the vehicle and when the girls were back inside their apartment, giggling like madwomen, Ritu had the last word.

'Aditya Shenoy,' she pronounced adopting a wise air, 'is a keeper.'

'Because his father owns a Lambo?' asked Aditi raising a sceptical eyebrow but Ritu refused to discuss the matter further and went off to her room.

~

Aditi's birthday dawned nice and pleasant, not too hot, not too rainy; Bangalore was pulling its old balmy number, and she was thankful for that. She lay in bed looking at the glowing scarlet blooms of the gulmohur outside her bedroom window, the sun dappling the branches, leaves and the flowers in a delightful manner. It felt good to be alive, she thought contentedly.

On cue, her phone played its jazz riff and she picked it up. It was her brother.

'Hi Addy,' he said, 'Many happy returns of the day.'

'Thank you,' she said sleepily.

'Still in bed, lazybones?' he asked, only half-joking. Akshay hated the idea of people wasting the early hours of the day lying in bed. He was a lark personified, woke up at what was to his younger sister the unearthly hour of 5 a.m., and generally got a good start on the day, well before most people were up.

They lazily exchanged news. Akshay ran a string of outlets in the more remote reaches of the Wayanad district that sold tribal handicrafts as well as organic herbs and food products. He had adroitly ensured the elimination of the ubiquitous middleman without stepping on any toes. The brand had really taken off during the last three-four years and now its stoles, soaps and tribal jewellery were sold across India. Akshay Pillai was much loved and almost deified by the tribals living there.

'What are plans for the day?' he asked her now.

The opportunity to yank his chain was too good to miss. 'Oh, I'm going to laze in bed as long as I can, it is a Sunday after all,' Aditi told him, tongue-in-cheek but he refused to take the bait, chuckling instead. She added, 'Then I'll help Ritu prep the place.'

'Party tonight?' her brother asked.

'Yup,' she confirmed happily, then asked, 'What's going on in your love life?'

There was a moment's nonplussed silence, then Akshay burst out laughing.

'Who told you turning twenty-nine allows you to ask such personal questions?' he queried and she smiled. Akshay was a terrific looker and there had been a time when his mother and sister had had to fend off all comely comers, purely because Akshay had no interest in them. That was then; now, he lived and worked in hamlets and the women in his family, his mother, his many aunts, older cousins, every interfering member of his family with the sole exception of his sister, wished he would find someone and get married so he wouldn't be alone up in the hills. Not that Akshay Pillai seemed anything but happy with his life.

He turned the tables on her. 'What about you? What's going on in *your* love life?' he asked.

But she was Aditi, not Akshay. She didn't play games. 'Oh, my boyfriend will be coming to the party tonight,' she informed him sunnily.

There was a moment's beat while he digested the news. 'Is it serious? What's his name? How long have you been dating him?'

Exactly the same set of questions her mother threw at her later in the morning, with an added one: is he a Malayali? And unlike her brother, her mother was not easily fobbed off.

Her mother forever lived in hope, reflected Aditi with rueful amusement. Neither of her offspring were stepping up to the plate, her set plate of expectations that is, but Mrs Pillai was sure that matrimony, then children, in short, a settled life, was waiting just around the corner for both her son and daughter.

But Aditi really and truly loved her mama, so she patiently replied, 'No Ma, he's Mangalorean. And it's very casual. Don't worry, I'll tell you if it gets serious.'

Her mother sighed gustily, dramatically, then got onto familiar ground. 'Aditi, how long will you carry on like this? If you are seen around Bangalore with all these boys, you'll acquire a name and...'

The birthday girl burst out laughing. 'A name for what, Ma? For going out with boys? For heaven's sake!'

'But nothing has really changed, Addy,' her mother earnestly assured her. 'Malayali mothers are still looking for good Malayali girls with curly hair (check, interjected Aditi irrepressibly), a sound knowledge of the language (half-check, went Aditi again), a girl who will go out and work but will run the household smoothly, cook, look after her husband…'

'…produce children at regular intervals, see to her in-laws when they come on long visits, keep out the Vishu kani, make a full-course sadya for Onam, stay in touch with all her relations, visit all her husband's relations; yes, Ma, I know, I know, you've been telling me this since I was, what, twelve?'

As she had intended, that got an indignant response from her mother who spluttered, 'Since you were twelve? Are you mad? It's just that you are getting on in years…'

Aditi had no wish to engage her mother in yet another fruitless discussion and she drew a deep exasperated breath. Then her father took the phone from his hectoring wife's hand and wished his daughter a happy birthday. 'Shall I get you the latest iPhone, molu?' he asked anxiously. Mr Pillai's affection for his daughter took the form of swamping her with gifts whether she wanted them or not.

'No, Pa, please no. I'm not a fan of the iPhone and I love my Chinese model,' she assured him. 'Then what do I get you?' he asked fretfully. 'Oh, hmmm, let's see, tell you what Pa, give me a day or so and I'll revert with a long list of stuff I need!'

He laughed but rang off only after securing a promise that she would send her list as soon as she could. There was going to be no list of course but just to indulge him, she would ask for something that would please him no end to gift her. What that was though, she had no idea…

She was still in bed sipping coffee and chatting with Ritu who had brought her the coffee when Aditya rang. Winking at Ritu, she picked up the phone.

'Many happy returns of the day, Aditi,' he said softly, and she exhaled.

'Thank you,' she replied equally softly.

'Confession time,' he told her wryly. 'I didn't know it was your birthday till the invite for this evening fetched up in my inbox, so I owe Ritu one.'

'Mmm,' she said, 'don't worry, she'll collect! Come early?'

'Will do,' he replied. 'Can't wait to see you,' he added and rang off.

But he didn't fetch up early. The small apartment soon filled up with people, Ritu's workmates as well as the Snack Team trio, and Aditi's other friends. The smokers were out in the small patch of garden, fouling up the air in Aditi's unstated opinion; those who wanted to listen to the music were sitting on the yak-skin rug and arguing their heads off. That the discussion had to do with retro music Aditi gathered from references to Bob Dylan, Johnnie Lee Hooker, Stevie Ray Vaughan...and Lady Gaga! One of her friends from Zumba class, a bright little thing with the most flexible bones ever, was demonstrating the art of twerking to a very interested bunch of guys and Aditi grinned. Paddy really could be effortlessly outrageous!

One of their favourite catering services had come up trumps and the food, mostly finger food, was going down a treat. The bar was manned by Mickey who threw her a cheerful wink every time she passed him by.

The flat had fairy lights wound around just about anything, the sofa backs, the table legs, acting like swags across the curtains, over the bookshelves, even artfully wound around the detested water fountain. The effect was magical. Out in the garden, they had lit votives, placed them in neon-coloured metal lanterns and hung them from whichever branch was stout enough to support the lanterns. There were steel buckets filled with red lilies, and it made for a dramatic touch.

Aditi was positively sparkling and the crowd seemed to be circling her, people coming and going but keeping her at the centre. Ritu had broken the bank and got her a crinkled silk designer skirt the colour of wine, hemmed with gold zari. Aditi had paired the skirt with an aquamarine halter silk top, piled on her usual kilos of silver, switched up her nondescript nose-pin for a silver one that held a wine-coloured stone in its centre. She did not wear a watch and refused to look at the wall clock in the dining area but she was fully aware that the party was well on its way and there was no sign of Aditya Shenoy. If Ritu and Mickey shared similar thoughts, their faces didn't reveal that for a minute.

In a spirit of—mistaken—bonhomie and charity, Aditi had decided to call a man she'd briefly dated and of course, Abhishek Mukherjee had turned up, he never said no to parties. He'd come with the latest bimbette type he was dating, one in a long line; Aditi had been proud to buck the trend, to be the only (very brief) exception to his penchant for pouting model-types whose interests generally ran to Justin Bieber and OTT clothes. Then again, she had quickly found Abhi was a profound bore, so maybe the bimbettes suited him better than a woman who knew and spoke her mind. His date for the evening, Mona Something, was no different; she teetered around the apartment in bright orange heels with a bored expression on her face. What was strange was that Abhi, after having brought her here, was pretty much ignoring her and trying to hit on the birthday girl instead. Aditi was an old hand at warding off the pompous man but she did feel sorry for Mona who clearly was not Mona Darling for him, not for this evening at least.

The music changed; obviously Rajat, Ritu's office colleague and Aditi's friend, who was handling that side of things, felt it was time for people to get on the floor. 'Shall we dance?' asked Mickey, looking at his wife Minu. Minu was in her usual form-fitting salwar suit and it suited her, showed off her curvy figure to perfection. Abhi got up and came towards Aditi with an owlishly determined expression on his face; she cringed inwardly but just in the nick of time, one of Ritu's colleagues moved in front of her and pulled her to her feet.

Aditya was not going to turn up. Swallowing the intense disappointment she felt, Aditi threw herself into the spirit of things and began to move provocatively, circling her delighted partner, tossing her curls with abandon. The fake-it-till-you-make-it adage came true and soon, the birthday girl was thoroughly enjoying herself. She pirouetted lightly on her jutti-shod feet and was caught up in a pair of arms, the feel of which she recognized immediately.

'Happy birthday, Aditi,' intoned her boyfriend and she looked up at him, her heart in her eyes. He bent his head and for a minute she wondered wildly if he intended to kiss her in front of all the very interested people present but instead, he just kissed her cheek softly. There they stood, caught inside a bubble all their own; he opened his mouth to say something but it was drowned in a loud, ecstatic shriek.

It was Mona, bearing down on Aditya determinedly, no trace of anything remotely resembling boredom on her face now. 'Aaaahditya Shhhhenoy,' she trilled and gave him a smacking kiss. On the mouth, Aditi noted sourly. He looked distinctly taken aback, then recovered his characteristic cool.

'Mona Dutta,' he said, smiling down at her. 'Long time! How have you been?'

And to the birthday girl's dismay and disbelief, the next minute, Abhishek Mukherjee's bimbette pulled Aditya into a corner and engaged him in some sort of intense talk. Aditi tried to mask her fury, caught Ritu's comical expression and immediately felt lighter in spirit. Hey, it was *her* place, and she could kick Mona Darling out any time she chose.

It was bitchy but she had to do it. When she next came upon Abhi, she asked in dulcet tones, 'How does it feel to have your girlfriend abandon you for another guy so obviously?' and earned a sulky look for her pains. Mona was unfortunately all too clearly just a casual date for Abhi but he didn't relish being shown up like this. 'Just who is that fellow?' he asked. She chuckled, saying, 'Only the owner of the Caboyea company', and that deflated him effectively.

However, Aditi's effervescence was fast fading as the night wore on and she found she couldn't get a minute alone with her so-called boyfriend. If he was really her boyfriend he ought to be sticking to her like glue, right? One thing she noticed though, he had managed to shake off Mona Darling and he spent quite some time chatting with Raman, Pia and Mickey. Aha, now that was good, thought Aditi with some satisfaction, moving closer to them.

'Is that an It bag?' Aditya asked a startled Pia, indicating the blood-red bag she had on her arm. Then he threw a wink at his girlfriend and told Pia in all seriousness, 'I have taken a crash course in It bags.' Ritu had taken him around the room introducing him to people, something Aditi felt *she* should have been doing. However, Aditya seemed to know a few of the people gathered there, and looked most comfortable.

Was he ignoring her, she thought on a sudden note of annoyance. That wasn't true, however; every time he came in Aditi's way, she got a very special smile, a smile that promised much. 'Short on delivery though,' Aditi found herself telling him at one point, almost as if they had been in a conversation.

'What?' he mouthed above the music.

'Nothing. Tell you later,' she replied and flounced away, aware that he was watching the sway of her pert bottom, taking in the view of her smooth back afforded by her halter top. She went into the kitchen to bring out the lemon chiffon pie, which was her choice of dessert. It had been lovingly baked by her aunt in Jakkasandra and brought over by her uncle who had stayed only for a cup of coffee and two cracker biscuits, then rushed back home. She had insisted there be no cake-cutting on the pain of death, and reluctantly her friends had agreed. Aditi had a decided aversion to birthday cakes being cut, candles being blown and people singing, all the more so if *she* was the birthday girl. 'Strange bird,' Mickey had grumbled but Minu said peaceably, 'A birthday girl is entitled to get what she wants,' and that had settled the issue.

'Put that cake down for a minute,' Aditya said from behind her. She turned slowly and asked him, 'Why?'

'So I can wish you properly,' he said and came purposefully towards her.

Obediently, Aditi put the cake down on the table and turned, lifting her face up to him. Her choice of a frosted pastel lipstick made her lips pop, look even more full, and he studied the provocative pout of those lips.

But he didn't kiss her immediately.

'Lovely, lovely Aditi,' he said on a fervent note. Then he took her lips almost savagely, which surprised Aditi. Aditya rarely lost control in this manner. She stayed surprised only for a moment though, then she wound her arms tightly around his neck and kissed him back. If he was desperate to take her in his arms, well, she had been desperate to be in them.

The kiss went on for what seemed to be a long time till they heard Ritu's voice dripping sarcasm. 'Hey guys, wanna come up for air? The dessert is actually a cake. On the table next to you. Not each other.'

They broke free, smiling into each other's eyes. Aditya picked up one of the mini tacos and slipped it into his mouth, closing his eyes in appreciation. 'What's in here?' he asked and Aditi beamed. She liked a man who was interested in food. 'Creamed mushrooms with spinach and chicken, it's the non-veg version you are having. Just spinach, mushrooms with corn for the vegetarians,' she told him.

'The birthday girl made it,' Ritu informed Aditya. 'With her own two hands.'

He grinned and said, 'Wow! My girlfriend can cook.'

'Very well, in actual fact, thank you,' Aditi informed him saucily. Then realized she'd walked into it when he said softly, 'A girl of many talents. And modest with it.'

Ritu heard and laughed. 'You must tell me about these talents,' she told him. 'Then I'll tell you stuff. About her.' Aditi made a face at them and carried the cake off to the dining table.

Later, much later, when there were just a handful of people around, all doing their own languid thing, Aditi and her boyfriend sat on the divan and he took out a small flat box, her birthday gift. Curious and more than a bit uncomfortable, devoutly praying it wasn't some expensive jewellery because she really wasn't that kind of girl, she opened the package to find a charming opal pendant with a kind of abstract pattern on its façade. She shot him a look of enquiry and he smiled.

'The lines go off into nothingness and come back from another side to rejoin the matrix,' he said, one long finger tracing the pattern. 'It's Aditi.'

'Aditi?' she asked, really intrigued now.

'Aditi. Limitless in Sanskrit. Mentioned repeatedly in the Vedas.'

She gulped, moved but not knowing what to say, then whispered, 'What a thoughtful gift.'

'Mmm,' he assented smiling mischievously. 'I spend a lot of time thinking about you.'

Now she was back on familiar ground and she gave a throaty chuckle. Leaning into him, she said, 'Someone once told me Aditi was the mother to all cows.' She kept a straight face for a minute or two, then burst into a fit of giggles. Aditya seemed much taken with that, chuckling.

Suddenly turning serious as a thought struck her, she asked him, 'Why do you and your father have different surnames?' She didn't know if this was the right time and place to ask such questions, most probably it wasn't, but she needed to know.

'Long story,' he said easily but there was no missing the reluctance to engage on this topic. 'Shenoy is my maternal grandfather's name.'

But Aditi was having none of this subterfuge. 'Maternal grandfather?' she asked, shooting him a direct look. 'And where do your maternal grandparents live?' She knew better than to pretend total ignorance about his mother. That would have seemed disingenuous.

'They live in a little coastal village near Udupi,' he told her. Then he stopped and fell quiet. Aditi waited patiently. There was no rushing him.

Eventually he heaved a deep sigh. 'My family status is quite complicated. Actually, I'm quite fond of my stepmother, too. She lives abroad.'

Aditi was dying to ask 'With her Argentinian boyfriend?' but bit her lip. If he wanted to tell her, he would.

He obviously did want to. 'She lives with her husband in London. He is from Argentina, a cattle rancher turned businessman. I'm quite close to her but I don't see much of them because I detest that fellow. Foolish and flashy as dammit.'

Aditi grinned, though she was actually more than confused by the complex dynamics of his family situation. 'Wow,' she said, choosing to focus on the woman's husband for obvious reasons. 'He's foolish as well as flashy?'

Aditya gave her a strained smile. 'He is. And pompous to go with it. I can't imagine what she sees in him.' Which made one thing clear to his girlfriend: he really liked his stepmother. Strange situation, strange family.

Then he lapsed into a deep silence but it was not a loaded one. He had withdrawn into his quiet shell and she was okay with that. They sat comfortably side by side, Aditi threading her fingers through his. After a while, she asked him softly, 'Feeling better?'

He got what she meant and smiled one of his killer smiles at her. 'Yes.' That's all he said but his eyes spoke volumes and she could read everything in there.

'How old are you today?' he asked, and she pretended to throw him a punch.

'You don't ask a girl her age,' she informed him crossly but he said, 'Yes, you do, if the girl is your girlfriend.'

'Well, if the girl is your girlfriend, you ought to know already.'

'Nope, one knows nothing until one asks,' he retorted, his fingers playing a sensual tattoo on the inside of her wrist, sending shivers of delight up her arm.

She told him and he raised an eyebrow. 'You look...' he began.

'…younger,' she finished. 'I get that all the time,' she told him a trifle smugly, and he chuckled.

'And how old are you?' she asked him, looking him straight in the eye, just as if she had not found out his age online. He smiled and said, 'Thirty-one.' Then cocked an eyebrow as if waiting for her to say something. Which she did but it wasn't a comment on how young he looked for his age.

'So. How exactly do you know Mona Darling?' she asked, trying to keep her voice matter-of-fact. Mona had left Aditi's party quite reluctantly, in a hilarious volte-face from the manner she had adopted at the start, blowing a series of kisses to a patently disinterested Aditya and cooing, 'We must meet later, darling.'

'Mona Darling?' he asked in an astounded tone, then almost immediately caught on and began to laugh.

'Bitch,' he told her lovingly, his voice a caress and she looked reproachfully at him, blinking her long lashes.

'Language, dude,' she told him reprovingly. 'No, but seriously…?'

'We used to play squash together at the club.'

'She plays squash?' Aditi asked him, an image of the other girl's perfect figure in shorts and a figure-hugging polo shirt coming into her head.

'She used to play squash. Now I wouldn't know. We haven't met in years. Her father and mine are business associates. She's sweet but well, a little…'

'…dumb,' finished Aditi helpfully and he grinned but didn't deny it. 'I thought you knew her from some Tinder-swiping,' she said, slanting him a look of pure mischief. He refused to rise to that bait and told her lazily, 'I don't do Tinder. Or Aisle. Or OkCupid. Or iBluebottle…'

'Really?' she asked him in her best arch manner. 'Then how is it that you know all their names? Surfing sites on lonely nights, eh? A clandestine left/right-swiper?' And she proceeded to dig him in the ribs. He feinted, then started to tickle her, leading Aditi to shriek with laughter and collapse on him.

Settling down, she raised a hand to stroke his jaw just as Ritu walked into the room. In a little set-piece of her own, as she told Aditi later, Ritu had spent most of the evening fending off Rajat. It was common knowledge that he carried a torch for Ritu (a whole damned mashaal, he'd said once, mocking himself) but she wasn't interested. Then again, quite like Aditi's mother, Rajat too lived in hope; the former for her daughter, the latter for himself.

'Yugaiz! Still at it?' Ritu asked in mock disgust.

'Still at nothing, Ms Bossy-boots,' Aditi replied, not bothering to snatch her hand back from her boyfriend's face. 'Let me remind you, I'm the birthday girl and I get to do whatever I want.'

'Whoa,' said an amused Mickey from behind Ritu. Minu and he came into the room, pulled large cushions and settled down on them.

'We really ought to leave,' Minu reminded him even as she made herself more comfortable. Aditi showed them the beautiful pendant Aditya had got her and there were exclamations of admiration all around.

'How's work going?' Aditya asked Mickey who shrugged and said, 'Ah, good days, bad days. It's a fast stagnating market but contrarily enough, the goalposts are constantly being moved. Our USP is basically fresh, local and minimally processed food, local snacks tweaked up, so we experiment with holige, nippattu and the like. Sometimes I think the Snack Team sits in the intersection between sardine tapas and drumstick bhajjis! But healthy snacks, believe it or not, continue to take a backseat, and all change on that front is still incremental. Still, it's interesting to see what people like and devour as snacks. What about you?' he asked Aditya.

'Well, I could say the same,' Aditya mused. 'A few good days, then a string of bad days. These aren't good times for cab aggregators. Government interest crosses into governmental interference all too easily—that's the tricky part. And the challenge is to open up job opportunities, hire quality staff and keep incentivising them while trying to stay in the black, make your profits but reduce congestion...yes, exactly,' he broke off laughing as Mickey said something short and unprintable.

'What's your edge?' Mickey asked, shooting the other man an intent look.

Aditya paused to consider that, then said, 'Well, I don't know that you could call it an edge. What my partner and I have is a simple, fluid model. We keep it small. We buy the cars, install GPS tracks, panic buttons, fare meters, bill printers. Then we scan a whole lot of applicants before hiring a limited set of drivers. Small enough in numbers so we know them personally and can vouch for them, and also make sure they don't hit the roads when they are drunk or exhausted.'

He then took a deep breath and said simply, 'It works for us. We will never cut into the profits of the big aggregators in a serious way but that doesn't matter. People like their cab-experience with us and become repeat customers.'

Mickey immediately picked up on that. 'It doesn't matter because you guys have deep pockets?' he asked, his earnest expression indicating that he wasn't being sarcastic or trying to bait the other man.

'Ha!' Aditya said on a laugh. 'I wish! But no, it's that we work to a set fiscal plan and so far we have had nothing to worry about.

'There are problems aplenty, of course. Data with aggregators constitute a threat of breach of privacy. So electronic records must be kept safe. Then the pricing ruckus is pitting the industry perpetually against the government. I'm not...' he said but Aditi impetuously cut in here.

'Well, I think the whole pricing thingie is a conspiracy against us poor passengers,' she pronounced. Aditya didn't argue but said sombrely, 'Everyone has their own compulsions.'

'Compulsions? To retain the drivers, you mean,' Aditi began spiritedly only to catch the meaningful glance thrown her way by Mickey, and subsided. The glance clearly said, 'Stop arguing with your boyfriend on your special day, you nut.' This argument could wait for another day, Aditi decided, then suddenly remembered that Aditya was against surge and other kinds of over-pricing, anyway!

'Aditi and you go back a long way, don't you?' Aditya now asked Mickey and she pricked up her ears. Aha, was this jealousy? But no, he was on altogether another track. 'How do you convert a friendship into a working relationship? Without scarring both, I mean?' he asked.

Mickey and she exchanged glances; they got this question from time to time.

'It's all good,' Mickey explained. 'We have each other's backs. Our disagreements never ever become personal attacks. There's the ease of old habits and rituals. We play fair because we care. For each other and for our shared business.'

'And that goes for all four of us,' Aditi said. 'Pia and Raman too.'

Just then Raman and Pia came through the French windows, both looking a bit flushed. Raman went to sit on a moda rather like a surly schoolboy while Pia started to talk into the air, brightly, meaninglessly.

'Shall I get everyone coffee?' Ritu asked, more to break Pia's stream-of-consciousness prattle, and everyone except Aditya said they could use a shot of strong java. 'I've got to go,' he said reluctantly and rose from the low divan.

Aditi walked him to the front door. And being Aditi, she had to ask. 'Why were you late?'

He grimaced ruefully. 'A small problem at work. Took some time to sort it out. Sorry…'

'I really like this apartment of yours,' he then told her, casting an appreciative glance about him. 'Tonight it looks wonderful. Does your landlord live in the vicinity?'

Aditi laughed. 'Our landlord is Ritu's father. They live in Malleswaram, so he's the ideal absentee landlord. In any case, they are very chilled-out folk. But both Ritu and I insist on a signed lease agreement and paying rent.'

'Okay,' he said, then pulled her gently to him, lifted away a thick rope of curls from her cheek, and dropped a kiss on the top of her ear. It was as unexpected as it was sensual and her ear started to tingle. 'Bye, love,' he said and then he was gone.

Aditi went back into the living room and sat by a now forlorn Pia, dropping her head onto the other girl's shoulder. 'What happened, Pia?' she asked softly under the cover of general conversation. Raman was telling Mickey how he'd been stuck at the notorious Silk Board Junction for almost three hours. It was arguably now the worst spot to traverse in all of Bangalore and Mickey responded sympathetically.

'I don't really know,' Pia told her, large brown eyes opening wide. 'We were smoking in the garden and I told Raman that my next-door neighbour—that lawyer guy?—was hitting on me. Then he erupted! Raman, of all people, would you believe it? Told me I was encouraging that man!' She laughed helplessly, the hurt showing and Aditi groaned in her mind. Raman sure was making a hash of things. Then Pia said, 'As if! I mean, the guy calls everyone "buddy". Men and women. Sometimes, me too.'

This fascinated Aditi. A wannabe lover who called the girl of his dreams 'buddy'?

'My mistake,' Pia informed her solemnly, running a hand over her blue-tinted hair. 'I should not have confided in Raman.'

'No?' asked Aditi.

'No, because he's some kind of straitlaced…uncle!'

The girls erupted into giggles which the others in the room studiously pretended not to hear, though Aditi noticed the tips of Raman's ears turning bright red.

After everyone had left, Ritu and Aditi efficiently did the basic clearing-up; their maid Kala would do the rest tomorrow. This was a routine the two girls had perfected through practice. One picked up and carried the used glasses to the sink; the other emptied ashtrays of those idiots who smoked inside. One of them emptied any remaining snacks from the bowls; the other packed leftover food into containers and stashed it away in the fridge.

'Good party,' Ritu asked, flicking an affectionate glance Aditi's way.

She beamed. 'Very good party. We stayed true to our creed.'

The girls had a simple but effective creed that their entertaining should be frequent and fearless. This had proved to be a hit formula, each time, every time.

CHAPTER SEVEN

Over the next few weeks, work pressures continued to mount on Aditi and the Snack Team. Two members of their already small transport fleet quit to join a leading cab company's new bike-taxi venture. One long-time client decided not to renew his annual contract with them. Their landlord came calling and that was always a bad thing because he never sought them out, except to demand a raise in rent.

The team did much brainstorming and developed some ideas to further power the business. They decided fresh pitches needed to be prepared and made, both to existing clients as well as potential new ones. They decided to outsource the job of hiring a transport team to a start-up that promised to do it efficiently. They decided to use Insta-illustrations to advertise the Snack Team. And then Aditi decided to go visiting some of her chef friends in town; it was time to draw up a new menu, one that would match the new pitch, word for word, taste for taste.

Aditya and she met as often as they could, which was mainly on the weekends now. He seemed to be quite tied up too, from what he told her, and it wasn't only business. His mother was in hospital with a severe case of dengue fever.

'She is so weak, it hurts to see her. She is precious to me. To all of us.'

'Who is all?' Aditi asked but she could hazard an educated guess. And she was right too, because he said, 'You've met my brother, Raj, the "real" Raj KS? And Preetha, his wife?'

'Ah, so that's who she is!' exclaimed Aditi. He stared at her for a moment and she explained. 'When we met at your apartment, you told Preetha who I was but you didn't tell me who Preetha was.' He smiled but didn't respond to that, it seemed petty for Aditi to blow it up, and anyway, the incident had taken place ages ago.

'Shall I come visit your mother?' she then asked, a trifle hesitantly and was immediately heartened by the warm note in his voice when he said, 'Of course. I'll take you to meet Amma when you get untangled from all those noodle strings.'

'What a pj, dude,' she chuckled, even as she wondered whether he would really take her to see his mother. Aditya seemed to prefer keeping his life compartmentalized: work, family, girlfriend, all in separate boxes.

'Want to meet Mandeep Oberoi?' he suddenly asked her over the phone the next night.

Mandeep Oberoi was the city's newly arrived wunderkind chef. He had trained under Paul Bocuse in Lyon, had done stints at a couple of Michelin-starred restaurants in New York City, then come home to Bangalore where his armyman father had settled down, to start his own restaurant out on Kanakapura Road. Aditi had never been but had heard that it had all the easy vibes of an East Village eatery, casual but elegant, and that it served up some really marvellous food which made the long drive out there totally worth it. But Chef Oberoi, from all accounts, also possessed an attitude that entered the room well before he himself did. She'd heard stuff about him. So, understandably enough, Aditi was not exactly dying to meet the man.

'Really?' she asked, hesitantly. 'Meet him and mine him for what…aperitif ideas?'

'No silly, his panzenella is quite popular, isn't it?'

'Panzenella! Full marks to you, Aditya Shenoy,' his girlfriend said, laughing.

'I hate polenta of any kind but he makes some amazing polenta, and I find myself eating it by the plateful,' he told her. 'Mann's an old friend of mine.' (*He would be*, Aditi thought waspishly to herself, rather unfairly). 'Go meet him, chat a while, see what ideas are thrown up…take Raman along too.'

It sounded good. She knew Raman would be over the moon with delight when he heard this.

'Alright. When?'

'Let me speak to Mandeep and lock on a date,' Aditya told her, then rang off with his usual: 'G'nite, love. Sleep tight, dream of me.'

~

It was Ritu, of course, who belled one particular cat. They were at their favourite burrito place in Indiranagar one night when she asked Aditi, 'Tell me, does the money thingie ever enter your equation with Aditya Shenoy?'

Aditi didn't pretend not to understand. She tapped her teeth reflectively with her spoon, making her friend roll her eyes in exasperation, then replied, 'Would you believe it? No. He doesn't dress too fancy as you know, he doesn't do an Edward Lewis.'

'Who is Edward Lewis?' interjected Ritu with a totally baffled expression.

'Richard Gere's character in *Pretty Woman*? Jetting her off to the opera in Paris, and such romantic acts, I mean.' She looked tranquilly at her friend who had gone into convulsions of merriment.

'Wow, you are seriously wacko!' gasped Ritu when she could finally speak. 'You are now comparing yourself to Julia Roberts. How exactly?'

Aditi put on an earnest look. 'Well, obviously not the hooker angle,' she explained in a kind manner which set off her friend again.

'I'm relieved,' Ritu butted in but Aditi let that go and continued, 'I meant a pretty woman dating a very rich dude…that kind of situation.'

'And now you are calling yourself a pretty woman. Why stop at that? Why not make it a beautiful woman?' Ritu eyed her in a snarky fashion but Aditi inclined her head graciously, and said, 'No, that would be way too immodest of me.'

But she returned to the topic, this time more seriously.

'Aditya wears top-quality stuff but it's all very discreet. He rides a Ducati and for all your telling me he has a garage full of bikes, I've seen only the Ducati, it's one he's had for many years. We don't talk about Sudarshan Kamath. And when he talks about Caboyea, it's mostly about how tough it is to stay in the black.'

'Which it is,' Ritu informed her smugly. 'Staying in the black, I mean. I Googled.' She ignored Aditi's muttered, 'The eternal Googler' and continued, 'Caboyea is a start-up which is chugging along well. For now.'

'Yes but he works hard for the money, Nosey Parker,' Aditi assured her.

'Does he pick up the tab on your dates?' Ritu asked in all seriousness.

Aditi paused to think. 'Not all the time,' she replied. 'I book stuff online often and I pay for it.' She realized she was relieved about this, even as she spoke.

But she meant what she told Ritu. Aditya being much richer than her didn't bother her one bit. In any case, while they were now dating exclusively, they hadn't talked of a future together and she sure was glad about that. Aditi was a certified marriage-phobe. She had seen enough marriages on the rocks to be wary of the institution, very wary. She had managed to evade all the pressure her mother put on her over the years, ever since she had turned twenty-five, in fact. She wasn't going to pressure her boyfriend for any kind of commitment beyond what they shared now. It was all good.

'Good for you,' Ritu said slightly wistfully when Aditi voiced her thoughts.

Aditi stared at the other girl curiously, a question in her eyes. As far as she knew, Ritu moved pretty much along the same trajectory as Aditi, dating casually without getting too involved in the relationship or with anyone. When it was time to move on, both girls retained the respect and in most cases the friendship, too, of their former boyfriends.

Ritu was avoiding Aditi's direct gaze now. 'Oh, I don't know,' she confided in a rush. 'Sometimes I feel…well, not lonely but definitely in need of a man, a serious relationship in my life.'

'Are your parents putting pressure on you, Rits?' asked Aditi even as she knew the answer.

'No, no, you know them, they are cool. It's me. Oh well, it's just a passing mood, I guess.'

Aditi knew better than to bring up Rajat's name; she knew for a fact that Ritu was not in the least interested in the lovelorn Rajat. As they got up to leave, Ritu said, 'Let me give you my two bits. If Aditya Shenoy is a keeper, I suggest you keep him.' She smiled but her eyes had a serious look.

On cue, Aditi asked in mock-horror, 'For keeps?' So far Aditya had steered clear of such talk but here was Ritu doing it on his behalf!

Two days later, Aditi was coming out after a client meeting on Vittal Mallya Road when someone hailed her. Not by her name, just a 'Hi!' She turned to see Preetha emerging from a high-end boutique.

Preetha came up to her and smiled pleasantly, 'It's…Aditi, right?' she asked. 'How have you been?' In the late afternoon sun Preetha looked positively luminous, her skin glowing, the exotic salt-and-pepper hair coiled in a thick, low bun at the nape of her neck. She wore an Eri silk sari the colour of a well-baked biscuit. She was lovely, her air of serenity settling like a gauzy wrap about her. Aditi felt awkward and inadequate, which for Aditi was a new experience.

'No shopping bag?' she asked Preetha.

'No, I work here,' Preetha told her and Aditi tried to mask her surprise. It appeared that Sudarshan Moneybags Kamath's family were all working types. None of them seemed to be living off the fat of his land, at any rate. Raj and Aditya worked at Caboyea and here was Preetha working in this posh boutique.

'Want to grab a coffee somewhere?' Preetha asked and Aditi assented. She never said no to coffee and well, she saw no harm in getting to know Aditya's sister-in-law better. They walked up to St Mark's Road and went into a popular café. Both opted for hazelnut cappuccinos. Leaning back in her chair, Preetha surveyed the other girl in a frank manner. Aditi didn't like that much but there was nothing she could do so she looked back expressionlessly, then decided to break the silence. She asked after Preetha's mother-in-law.

'Oh, Aditya told you about her?' asked Preetha, distinct surprise in her voice. 'Amma's home now but it's a slow road to recovery from dengue fever. She had a bad attack. We live with her but Aditya comes home every evening after his long workday just to check on Amma,' Preetha continued, her tone admiring.

'How is Raj doing?' Aditi asked. She had realized Preetha's visit to Aditya's apartment the other day had had something to do with Raj.

Preetha looked discomfited for a moment, then said, 'Raj is still in recovery,' without specifying just what the man was recovering from. She continued, 'There too, Aditya was like a rock. Just took charge when Raj had his meltdown.'

Then she leaned in, smiling at Aditi like a friendly but slightly dangerous cat. 'Aditya is totally devoted to us. In all matters, we come first for him. This is something I feel I should tell all his girlfriends, just so they don't suffer disappointments later.'

Ah, this was going to be that kind of catch-up coffee, Aditi thought, then she leaned in too, propping her elbows on the red-tiled table. 'So, do you?' she asked pleasantly.

Preetha looked nonplussed, loosening her bun and retying it in a casually fetching gesture. 'Do I what?' she asked Aditi blankly.

'Do you tell all Aditya's girlfriends that?'

Preetha had the grace to look shamefaced, but just barely. She gave Aditi a contrite smile and said, 'No, that was a stupid remark. Aditya hasn't had a long string of girlfriends.' Clearly that was all she was going to vouchsafe. Then she touched the back of Aditi's hand and said, 'And you are quite the prettiest of all his—few— girlfriends.'

This was evidently a make-good gesture. Aditi wasn't too amused but she saw that she was expected to respond so managed something of a strained smile.

'Oh dear, have I hurt your feelings?' asked the other woman, a genuinely stricken expression on her face.

Aditi said, 'No, you've just pissed me off a bit.' She stared hard at Preetha but the other woman didn't look away.

'But you don't need me to tell you that you are a lovely girl. *You* can tell *me* something instead. Are you serious about Aditya?'

'You want to know if I'm a player?' Aditi asked, fixing Preetha with a direct look. 'Since we have already established that your brother-in-law is not a player?'

Preetha laughed and the laugh was a jarring one. 'That's true. Aditya is no player, he's too sweet for that.'

Sweet. Yuck, thought Aditi, taking a sip of her excellent coffee.

Preetha continued, 'It's just that you are so young.'

Better to nip this in the bud, thought Aditi and said in a matter-of-fact tone, 'Not that young. I'm almost thirty.'

There was a look of surprise in Preetha's eyes. 'Really? You look so much younger,' her sweet tone almost made Aditi gag. But she wasn't going to let the other woman score points here, so she asked, 'So what were you about to say? That I'm too young for Aditya?'

Preetha slowly, deliberately took a sip from her cup and slowly put it down in its saucer, taking her time.

'No actually, I was going to say you are too young to be dating my brother for his money...'

'Oh!' Aditi exclaimed in an exaggerated way. 'Aditya has lots of money?'

Preetha sniffed. 'Please don't act disingenuous, Aditi. I'm sure you know that as Sudarshan Kamath's sole heir, he is a very rich man. Or will be.'

Aditi said as pleasantly as she could, 'I'm sure you won't believe me but I did not know that Aditya was his father's sole heir. Sudarshan Kamath does have two sons, right?'

'Oh, Raj fell out of the running years ago. You haven't done an online check on my father-in-law?' Preetha asked, the barb thinly disguised. 'Aditya gets chased by a lot of girls who well, what is the term…'

'I believe the term is gold-digger,' offered Aditi helpfully, now seething with anger.

'Yes, that's it, they are gold-diggers.'

'But with protective sisters-in-law like you around, I'm sure he comes to no harm,' Aditi delivered the hit calmly then continued, 'You know what, I think this coffee break has served its purpose. You have warned me off. I don't give a rat's ass about your warning, Preetha Kamath, Shenoy, or whatever your surname is. And no, I won't be talking to your brother about this, don't worry. Now I've got things to do, so bye.'

Preetha just sat back and chuckled, the sound of it making Aditi turn around in surprise. 'It's Preetha Shenoy, actually,' she said and continued, 'I really don't know why you are so prickly. It was nice chatting with you. And do please tell Aditya about our coffee…I am going to do so, anyway.'

Not quite knowing who had got the better of that slightly weird encounter, Aditi took a Caboyea car home and glowered so hard at the back of the poor driver's neck that the man looked nervously at her in the rear-view mirror all through the ride.

Since she had set out during the peak-hour traffic, it was a long ride. Ritu wasn't home and suddenly Aditi wanted to see Aditya and hear his voice so bad.

He picked up the phone at the first ring. 'Hi, sweetie,' he said sounding quite upbeat about something.

'Hi,' she replied and he immediately picked up on the glum note in her voice.

'All okay, Aditi?'

'Mmm,' she said. 'I just wanted to hear your voice. Are you too busy to come over?'

'I'm in a business meeting,' he replied and she could hear the buzz of voices, a woman's high-pitched laugh in the background. 'Meet you in a couple of hours' time?' he asked.

'No, it's okay,' Aditi replied tiredly. 'I'm so low on energy, I'll just crash. G'night.' And she clicked the phone off on his concerned, 'Aditi?'

Some time later she was bathed, wrapped up in her favourite, very ratty nightshirt, an outsized bowl of ramen gripped between her palms, and feeling heaps better. She hadn't been quite able to gauge the depth of Preetha's motives. So. What was Preetha anyway? Over-protective? Over-possessive? Over-weird?

Damn Preetha. She was not worth brooding over, Aditi decided just as the doorbell went.

It was Aditya on the other side of the door, of course, she should have known. Aditi could have died, intensely conscious of her gear, her fluffy pink bunny slippers and her scrubbed pink face.

But her boyfriend wasn't looking too hard at what she had on. He came in swiftly and swept her into his arms with an exuberance that wasn't typical of him at all. 'Aditi, Aditi,' he said and then kissed her. It was a kiss full of joy and passion. Aditi kissed him back and then she pulled back.

'Okay, you are on a high,' she told him. 'Why are you on a high? Have you been smoking something you shouldn't be smoking?'

He grinned boyishly, then said, 'Nope to the dope. That

Canadian conglomerate I told you about is seriously interested in weighing in with Caboyea.'

'Big money?' she asked him, catching his happiness like it was some infectious bug.

'Big money and big tech support,' he intoned solemnly, then picked her up and swung her around.

When he put her down, Aditi stared at him suspiciously. 'How much have you had to drink?' she asked him, for all the world like a possessive girlfriend.

'My usual two, that's all,' he told her then catching the drift, grinned. 'I'm not drunk, woman. But if you want, we can go and celebrate, get rip-roaring drunk.'

But Aditi was nothing if not an astute businesswoman. 'Have they signed on the dotted line?'

'Not yet but they will next month,' he told her.

'Then we will celebrate next month,' she said firmly but he wasn't listening. His attention was diverted.

'Wow,' he told her, his voice dropping, looking at her gaping neckline—the shirt had lost its first few buttons many moons ago—in such a way that Aditi turned a little more pink.

'You really are dressed for bed,' he murmured suggestively.

'I told you so,' she told him a little crossly.

The next minute, she was back in his arms and he was nuzzling her collarbone, making her shiver with delight. She thought she heard him murmur 'Darling, darling' but she was too dazed to be sure. He pushed the neckline of the shirt open and one hand went to her breast. After which, Aditi could not for the life of her hear or mishear him any longer. He ignited her. She moaned as he caressed her breast, his fingers light yet insistent. He kissed her again deeply and this time the intent was unmistakable.

Suddenly he lifted his head and asked, 'Where is Ritu?'

'Out,' she managed. Then truthfully and to her mind, stupidly, added, 'But likely to be back any minute now.'

His movement arrested, Aditya stood still for a moment. Then he relaxed and laughed, his laughter carrying a sharp edge to it.

'Boy, talk of mood-breakers,' he said. She felt like kicking herself; why on earth had she told him of Ritu's imminent return?

'But it can wait?' she asked him hopefully, her head cocked to one side like a curious robin.

He looked into her eyes and said, 'Yes, it can, it will wait.' The statement held a delicious promise.

'It's late, I'll get going,' he told her, refusing the offer of a nightcap.

At the door, he turned, suddenly remembering something and said, 'Preetha told me the two of you met for coffee.'

Wow, that was quick. Did she call him so often then? Aditi opened her mouth, saw his happy expression and subsided.

'Yes,' she said.

'Great,' he said, sounding quite content. 'I'm sure you'll like her when you get to know her better. She's terrific.'

Aditi chose to focus on the peripherals of that statement. 'It's important to you that we get on, Preetha and I?' she asked, a careful expression on her face.

He swept one thick swathe of curls off her brow, looked into her eyes and told her, simply, succinctly. 'Yes, it is. Very important.'

'Why?' Aditi asked and she wasn't being coquettish.

'Because Aditi Pillai, you are very important to me.'

'How important?' she asked, a catch in her voice. Her innate caution was slowly reasserting itself.

But Aditya Shenoy was back in control of himself. Dropping a tender kiss on her temple, he told her, 'More important than you can imagine. Good night, my love. Sleep tight and dream of me.'

And he was gone, just like that. But Aditi wasn't too hassled. Her cute cabbie boyfriend had just shown that he could and would step up to the plate when needed.

CHAPTER EIGHT

In a masterstroke of irony, when Aditya finally fixed up a lunch meeting with Mandeep Oberoi, Raman was not in town. He'd had to go to Patna because his mother had fallen ill and been hospitalized. Raman was an only son and took his responsibilities very seriously.

And so it was just Aditi and her notebook that made it to the sweet little restaurant tucked in a quiet lane, quite some distance away from Bangalore's busy roads and noisome traffic. She then proceeded to have the time of her life, tucking into superlative food created by the superlative Chef Mandeep, even as she was vastly entertained by the non-stop pearls of wisdom that he let drop, like he was some oracle of cuisine and people. Maybe Aditya had spoken to him beforehand because Chef M was quite charming and did not display one bit of the petulant behaviour he was known for.

More than three hours later, she entered the office and sank down in a happy stupor. Catching the curious glances thrown her way by the others, she gurgled in response. Which of course, had them rushing over to her table for a blow-by-blow account.

'Okay, where do I start?' Aditi teased. 'The café is lovely, all pinewood furniture, lemon-coloured chair seats and tablecloths and huge pots and pans, urns and wine flacons suspended from hooks in the ceiling.

'Chef Mandeep is very fair, very fat and I counted as many as five rings on his fingers! He talked and talked and talked…'

Registering the disappointment in the eyes on her, she finished, '…all the while cooking up a storm.'

'What did you get to eat?' asked Pia.

'What didn't I get to eat!' Counting theatrically off her fingers, Aditi began to enumerate. 'I had an amaze salad, a concoction of kidney beans, baby spuds, mushrooms and beet around fresh prawns draped lightly in mayo. I had the soup of the day, lentil soup, which was delicately laced with the most fragrant herbs from their in-house herbery…and I'll never quite look at dal soup in the same way again!

'Then I had spinach-spiked lasagna.'

Mickey grinned. 'You had what? You loathe spinach and detest lasagna!'

Her friends all knew how spinach was the stuff of her nightmares, a dislike formed when her mother used to thrust the greens down her throat when she was a child and as for lasagna, she actually had a history with lasagna; it had been a string of bummer relationships at most restaurants from Cuffe Parade, Mumbai to Carmel, California.

'But this was Chef Mandeep's spinach lasagna, guys, a clever folding of agnolotti stuffed with palak. It was so melt-in-the-mouth delish, I actually had two helpings!'

A rapturous look on her face, Aditi continued debriefing her captive audience. 'The main course was fish. Because I am a Mallu, said Chef M. The flesh was so tender, the butter that bound the fish sealed the flavour in an intense way, and I was almost weeping with ecstacy while eating it.'

'And the dessert?' asked a fascinated Pia.

'The dessert was the stuff of poetry, guys! A Mont Blanc pudding, the chocolate blended beautifully with chestnut puree, all of it topped by a curl of sour cream. I will be dreaming of that dessert for at least a month now, I promise you!

'And Chef Mandeep talked all the while, the sunlight catching the stones on his many rings and making them flash! It was damned distracting; was I to look at his face, look at my food or look at those glinting rings? He dished the dirt—with a lot of relish—on Bangalore's gliteratti, chatterati and poseurati, some of whom you know…all of which I'll tell you in installments over the many dinners you will take me out for!'

She then delivered the finale with a flourish. 'I didn't speak more than three sentences all through. There was no chance, and my mouth was kept busy simply eating the food. But when I was leaving, Chef Mandeep told me he had really enjoyed my conversation. That I had an informed mind and elegant wit.'

After the gales of incredulous laughter had subsided, Mickey asked, 'And what did you say to that?'

'Nothing,' Aditi said. 'I waved him an elegant goodbye and scooted. Elegantly!' And they fell to laughing again, Mickey, Pia and she.

'He didn't ask one question about our company! I think he thought I was a reporter,' Aditi told them.

'He sounds weird, this great chef,' Pia said, then asked, 'Did all this food have majorly exotic ingredients in it? Truffles, Ponzu mayonnaise, stuff cooked sous-vide and such?'

Aditi sat up. 'Would you believe it, no!' she told them. 'Turns out, Chef Mandeep scorns molecular gastronomy, he called it dramebaazi! I ate what we eat in upmarket Mediterranean restaurants around town. But I have to say this…' and taking a leaf out of Chef Mandeep's style, she paused for dramatic effect. Till Mickey dryly said, 'Cut the crap and tell us already!'

'His food tastes totally hatke! Some special twist to each and every dish.' At which the Snack Team resolved to go eat there at the earliest.

Mickey asked her, 'Did you get any food ideas at all from the three-hour lunch with our local El Bulli?'

'It was two hours, actually. And yes I did,' she happily told them. 'Mozzarelline fritte and pepperoni imbottiti. Gnocchi with stuffings of our choice. Further details when Raman returns.'

And they had to be content with that.

'What did you think of Mann?' Aditya asked her when he called her late at night.

Prompted by sheer mischief, Aditi pitched her voice to a calibrated gush. 'I found him sexy!' she exclaimed.

There was a moment's pause as her boyfriend tried to ascertain if she was kidding. Then he said cautiously, 'Sexy? Really?'

'Yes,' she exclaimed, then sighed gustily. 'It's the combination of a silver tongue and deft fingers…'

'Deft fingers?' Aditya asked sharply, and she grinned. 'You know what I mean. He was chopping, mincing, dicing, sautéing. I found the whole thing very…'

'Yes,' he said dryly. 'Sexy. You've already mentioned it.'

Aditi waited for him to blot his copybook. Which he did, after another moment's silence.

'You didn't think he was well, rather chubby? Back in the day, we used to call him Billy Bunter. You know, that fat schoolboy character…?'

She burst out laughing. Time to let him off the hook, she decided and gurgled into the phone, 'Yes, that he was. Podgy more than chubby.'

But Aditya was still following his own train of thought. 'And you found that sexy?' he asked her.

'No, I didn't, I was just yanking your chain,' she was still laughing. 'And you need to play your favourite Roxy music song now.'

This time he caught on quick. 'Jealous Guy?' he asked his voice raised in amusement.

'Well, you said it, not I,' Aditi told him sweetly.

'I wasn't acting like a jealous guy,' he told her ignoring her disbelieving snicker. 'It's just that some girls really do fancy Mann.'

'Well, I'm not one of them,' she assured him. 'I fancy quite another type of guy.'

'Really?' he asked, lowering his voice to a suggestive drawl. 'And what kind of guy do you fancy, Aditi Pillai?'

'Mmmm, let me see now. Tall, fit, with eyes the colour of midnight skies and the sexiest jawline ever.'

'Are you describing anyone I know?' he asked her, a teasing note mixed with something deeper in his voice.

'Actually, I am,' she told him happily. 'My boyfriend.'

He replied in all seriousness. 'I have a message from your boyfriend. It's a question, actually.'

'You do? What, what, what?' she asked, snuggling deeper in the bedclothes.

'He wants to know what you are wearing. Right now.'

'Oooh, now we are into phone sex, are we?' she giggled then said, 'Tell him that would be a pair of cotton short shorts, red and orange checks with...' and she trailed off.

'With?' he asked alertly.

'Well, it's a hot night…' again she trailed off.

'With what, woman?' he asked.

She relented and said, 'Down, boy! With just my bra.'

'And what colour is your bra?' he asked.

'What were you, a tracker dog in your past life?' she asked him. 'Not going to tell,' she added impishly.

'In that case, I might as well come over and see for myself,' he informed her and for one delirious moment, she believed him. Then he laughed softly and said, 'This needs to be taken to closure but I really gotta go. We are putting in some new directives for drivers tomorrow. It's going to take some effort, getting them to agree.'

~

Aditi woke up a few days later to find the steel flyover plan had broken over her head and the unsuspecting heads of Bangaloreans quite without warning. And of course, her phone rang constantly.

'What is it all about?' she asked an activist friend.

'The government is hell-bent on pushing a very expensive steel flyover, supposedly to reduce congestion on the road to the airport,' her friend told her. 'Apart from the fact that the costs are hugely disproportionate to the components of the bridge, what has got us really riled is that nearly a thousand old trees are to be axed in the process of building the flyover!'

By the end of the day, Aditi had been speaking with half the city it seemed, and a plan of protest was in place. It was to be a silent protest along the route of the proposed flyover, an effort to shame the government.

Mickey, for one, was less than impressed by the plan; he didn't think silent protests would cut any sort of ice with the authorities. 'Silent protest? Epic fail. Governments are brazen, it's their very character,' he mused as Minu, Aditi and he sat in his living room. Aditi had dropped in for a drink and stayed on for one of Minu's delicious dinners. It was a Thursday and Minu prepared only veggie food on Thursdays but Aditi didn't mind at all. She'd had a sneak peek at the menu and was satisfied with what she saw. There was masala bhindi, methi aloo, a yellow dal, and a Minu specialty, kadhi. The rotis were beyond soft and Aditi ended up eating more than she meant to, but then, she always did that at Mickey's place.

'Yes, but I'm not sure the very character of Bangalore is suited for violent protest,' she said.

'You are talking about the Bangalore of old, Addy,' he told her. 'Today, you'll get enough of a lumpen mob to turn up, should that be a requirement.' Turning to his wife, he started to tell her all about the Bangalore of old and drew such a nostalgic picture that Aditi, who too had grown up hearing tales of the city of yore, became wistful and pitched in, drawing from her own memory bank. Together, they told Minu about the Udayvan open-air restaurant on MG Road, the Lakeside ice-cream parlour where one got the best falooda ever; the original Corner House famed for its hot chocolate fudge; the charming atmosphere of the Victoria Hotel; the buzz on the old Agram race track on drag racing days. They told her about the old Plaza Theatre, the world's best bookshop ever called Premier, then reverted to food talk again, talking of restaurants like Blue Fox and Topkapi, which ran on as much pure atmosphere as great food.

'Wow!' exclaimed Minu. 'And you guys watched all these places get pulled down?'

The two raconteurs looked at each other and stopped in mid-flow.

'Not really,' said Mickey a trifle sheepishly. 'It's what we have heard our parents talk about!'

'We've seen a whole lot of pictures, too,' Aditi said in stout support of her friend. They shared a laugh at how they had really sounded like old-timers but there was no doubting that they were Bangaloreans committed to doing what they could for their city.

Then Mickey said, 'And today's picture of Bangalore? A sprawling network of potholed roads, heaped piles of garbage, stinking open drains, rampant and berserk construction activity covering every surface with lung-choking dust, way more vehicles than the roads can handle.'

'We did it to ourselves and we can still put things right,' Aditi said and Mickey nodded in sombre agreement. Then he changed tracks abruptly.

'So Addy,' he asked, 'How are things going with your boyfriend of the same name?'

Aditi lazily protested, 'We do NOT have the same name, you goof!'

'Whatever. Things good?'

She smiled happily. 'Yes. Very good.'

At which Minu asked, a little hesitantly, 'Are things serious between the two of you?'

She wasn't going to lie to Minu. She hesitated, trying to choose her words and Mickey cut in, 'Minu my sweet, you may not know this but our girl here is the original commitment-phobe.'

'Meaning?' asked Minu, a troubled frown marring her smooth brow.

'Meaning, Aditi will happily sail into relationships of the most superficial sort. She'll go dancing, drinking, dining, to the movies, to rock concerts with her boyfriends. Then, the moment they turn serious, she'll walk. Dump them as politely as she can. It's ta-ta, bye-bye.'

Minu looked at her. She looked back at Minu and shrugged. And then, to her surprise, Minu almost wailed, 'But why, Aditi?'

Somewhat taken aback by the other girl's intensity, Aditi was a bit discomfited, then pulled a face. 'Oh well, what can I say?' she told Minu. 'That's the way I am.'

'No but Aditya is such a sweet guy,' Minu insisted and now it was Mickey's turn to look uncomfortable. He had not seen his placid wife get so worked up. In a bid to ease things, he said, 'I gotta tell you, Minu, all Aditi's boyfriends so far have been dumb dudes. You remember meeting Abhishek Mukherjee at her birthday bash? One of her exes. And there's no saying Aditya Shenoy won't be one more in that long line.'

Aditi had to laugh at this. 'Oy! That's too much, Micks,' she protested. 'Call him what you like but I don't think Aditya's dumb.'

Minu pounced immediately. 'Then why are you so insistent on keeping things casual?' she demanded.

But Aditi knew just how to deflect what was becoming an intense conversation. 'Minu, my dearest Minu,' she said laughing, 'What makes you think Aditya Shenoy is serious about me?'

Which stopped Minu in her tracks. Chasing men just wasn't a done thing, not in her book. 'Anyone for paan?' asked Mickey and got up to go to the stall at the end of the street the moment the girls chorused 'Me!'

~

'Are you joining us in the *Flyover Beda* protest on Sunday?' Aditi asked her boyfriend. They had just finished watching a particularly bad Hindi film.

'Yes, if I can make it,' he replied, lightly picking up her hand and lacing his fingers with hers.

'Make time, na,' she pleaded. 'We need full-weight strength.'

He looked troubled. Looking into her eyes, he asked, 'Aditi, you really think a silent protest will stop the powers that be from doing what they want to do?'

'Don't be a pessimist!' she exclaimed and he shook his head but kept quiet.

Outside her apartment block, she asked, 'Are you coming up?' hoping he would say yes. But he didn't. Sometimes Aditya Shenoy drove her mad with his restraint, she decided.

'No, I have back-to-back client meetings starting early tomorrow,' he said. She took off her helmet and shook her curls free and he watched entranced. He put out a hand to stroke her curls, then said abruptly, 'I love your curls.'

Pleased and rather surprised, Aditi teased, 'Only my curls?'

But she had caught him in a serious mood. Not laughing in reply, he took off his helmet with a look of naked need on his face that made her heart race.

'No,' he said slowly. 'Not just your curls. I love your dimples, I love the way you throw your head back and laugh. I love your bindaas manner. I love the way you gesticulate with your hands. I love the glint of your nose-ring, the sound of your payals on the rare occasions you wear them. I love the way you cock your head to one side like a bird when you ask questions. I love the way you swear. I love the way you kiss…'

And here he stopped because Aditi launched herself into his arms and kissed him fiercely, full on the mouth. Luckily, it was late and the streetlight was as usual not working, because otherwise they would have drawn a full and appreciative crowd of gawkers.

She pulled away from him, opened her mouth to say something but quickly shut it again. 'See you on Sunday,' she told him breathlessly and scooted up to her apartment.

Just inside the door, she stopped and pressed a hand to her mouth. Because she realized she had been about to say 'I love you, Aditya Shenoy' to him.

'Control, control, Aditi,' she told herself sternly. Light and easy was the way she wanted to keep this; serious brought its own share of problems.

CHAPTER NINE

It was an exultant Monday at the office. Pia announced that they were doing very well and had passed the targets for the quarter with a whole month to go. The festive season was almost on them and so were a host of new orders, too. It was time to scale up, Mickey announced; maybe the tide had turned for them and they needed to act on it like, now!

'The decision to tie up with that transport company was a good one,' he proclaimed. 'Whose idea was it?'

Aditi was quick off the mark. 'Raman's,' she said sweetly and all three of them started to laugh.

Then Pia said, with a slightly self-conscious look on her face. 'Raman actually called me from Patna.'

Aditi didn't know what to say so she said nothing but Mickey waved a hand in the air and said, 'Of course he did.' Since both the girls just stared at him, he went on in a carefully casual voice, 'Pia, my dear girl, Raman's been crushing on you like, for years.'

Pia made a sound midway between a squeak and a gasp. Looking at her, Aditi could see that the idea had its merits. *Fingers crossed for you Raman*, she thought. And then they got down to work. Since they were between interns, of who they usually had two or three aboard, they had taken on a couple of people and were in the initial painful period of easing them into the Snack

Team's routine. The girl Anita was a quick study, ready and willing to learn and do. The boy Bobby, on the other hand, was rather slow on the uptake and downright scatty, though the green thatch (a bright green at that) down the front of his hair kept the 'seniors' secretly amused. His careless ways were getting on their nerves, though; Raman had a calmer temperament than all of them and they were hoping he would be able to tackle Bobby better.

'*Bangalore Days* wants to do a piece on us, guys,' Mickey told them. 'I suggested next week because Raman should be back by then.'

'Oh good, we could do with some publicity,' Aditi said even as Pia exclaimed, 'What do I wear?'

They looked at Pia.

'Sackcloth?' suggested Aditi dryly but affectionately even as Mickey said, 'Something sexy.'

Pia did not react to Aditi but gave Mickey a schoolteacher kind of look. 'Are you being sexist, Micks?' she asked severely. Mickey had the grace to blush and opened his mouth to reply but was saved by the sound of something breaking in the next room.

The three immediately turned to each other and laid bets on the culprit being Bobby. Then Anita came hesitantly into the room, pushing her specs higher on her nose and said apologetically, 'Sorry! The teapot slipped through my hand.'

Aditi shut her eyes. She was the one who had insisted they brew tea the old-fashioned way. After the initial protests, all of them made their many cuppas of green tea through the day in the teapot, which was a lovely bright orange one.

Typically, it was Pia who smiled reassuringly at the stricken Anita and told her, 'It's okay, Anita. It's just a teapot. We'll get another.'

Aditi was eating a hurried sandwich for lunch when her boyfriend called.

'Come meet Amma this Sunday?' he asked without preamble. 'Since the *Flyover Beda* protest has been pushed to next month?'

Aditi had clean forgotten she had offered to go meet the woman, literally in the heat of the concerned moment. Now she went hot, then cold, realizing this was not part of her plan at all. She didn't want to meet his family members, thus raising the intangible bar in any way. But how on earth was she going to refuse?

The silence stretched on and when Aditya spoke next, he sounded just a bit put off. 'Something the matter, Aditi?' Then he added dryly, 'Busy as ever?' Aditi decided she wouldn't run from this; instead, she'd handle whatever came her way when it came her way.

'No, I was busy swallowing my BLT,' she told him. 'Yes, I'm free.' Then, sounding rather like Pia, she asked, 'Must I wear a salwar-kameez or something?'

Aditya laughed his low turn-on laugh and she closed her eyes in bliss. 'Wear whatever you want,' he told her. 'You'll look lovely.'

Later on, Ritu seconded him saying, 'Wear whatever you want, Addy. In any case, you are not going on an official visit, are you?'

Aditi carefully considered that. 'I don't know what you mean by official visit,' she told her friend. 'I mean, Aditya hasn't proposed to me or anything.'

Ritu narrowed her eyes. 'And when he does propose,' she said enunciating each word carefully, 'you are going to run till you reach Mexico, right?'

Aditi had nothing to say to that. She looked searchingly over at Ritu but the other girl was not being judgmental, she was being honest.

'Look,' began Aditi, carefully choosing her words. 'I'm not leading him on or anything. He doesn't tell me much about his weird family situation…'

'Because you don't ask?' Ritu interjected.

'Well yes, I don't ask. But surely given that we are so close, he should be confiding in me a bit, right?'

'No, Addy,' Ritu said firmly. 'He's one of us, basically chilled-out but not too keen to talk about himself. He's not going to volunteer information if he feels the recipient is not too interested. Just like we wouldn't. He can sense the Lakshman rekha you have carefully set up. And he respects that. But I don't know if he likes it.'

Aditi considered that, eyes half-closed. Then she said as firmly as Ritu, 'Okay, you have a point. But let me assure you, Aditya Shenoy is not too bothered about that Lakshman rekha.'

Ritu had the last word though. 'Because,' she said, 'he is waiting for the right time to cross that line. And then what are you going to do?'

'Gonna cross that bridge only when I come to it, yaaas?' Aditi laughed.

But somewhat to Aditi's dismay, Ritu hadn't let go of the subject even the next day. They were going to a friend's book launch and emerged from their bedrooms into the living area to call for a cab. Both girls were firm Caboyea clients now.

Ritu asked casually, 'Tell me something, Addy?'

Bending at an awkward angle to slip on a pair of vertiginous stilettos, she asked 'What?'

'Where do you see yourself ten years down? Personally, I mean?'

Aditi considered cussing a blue streak at Ritu, just for the heck of it, then sighed loudly and dramatically. 'Really, Rits? We bloody well don't have the time for this.'

Ritu checked her phone and announced with some satisfaction, 'Yes, we do. Driver is about eight minutes away.'

Aditi relented. 'If you are—most unsubtly—asking whether marriage figures in my future, the answer is most probably not.'

'If I didn't know you better, I'd say you are this way because of some past trauma,' declared Ritu, shaking her head. 'But I do know better.'

Aditi shook her head, refusing to meet her friend's eyes. 'I really don't know what the fuss is about,' she said defiantly. 'I'm happy the way I am, I just don't want to be tied down to marriage, and you want to psychoanalyze this?'

'Down with the prickles, sweetie,' her friend said, grinning. 'I just think it's a bit odd.'

'Well, I don't,' Aditi retorted spiritedly. 'Marriage is not the be-all and end-all of things.'

Ritu put her head to one side and considered that. 'Oh-kay...' she said slowly. 'Then, in your opinion, what is?'

Aditi stared at her. 'Are you trying to get me worked up? Why should there be a be-all and end-all to marriage, to love, or to anything in life, dash it?'

Then on a note of pure inspiration, she asked Ritu, 'Do a head count of all our friends. How many of them are married?' She looked on smugly while the other girl was obviously going through a roster in her head.

They were in the cab when Ritu turned to Aditi and gasped, obviously continuing the earlier conversation, 'Just about six people!'

'Yup. That was my point,' Aditi smiled graciously in perceived victory, as she decided these crazy heels were the most uncomfortable thing she had ever worn in her life, even though it gave such an oomph factor to the pencil skirt she was wearing. However, having paid through her nose for the wretched pair, she would have to wear them a few times more before relegating them to the back of her shoe cupboard. Such are the woes of girls, she thought. Along with people who talked marriage at them continuously.

~

She decided to treat the home visit as a casual one and dressed accordingly in one of her vibrant skirts, a blue and green one which she paired with an off-white short top. Her usual quota of silver bangles, rings and large jhumkas completed the look. As she sprayed on her staple, Romance, she hoped like hell that the mode of transport today was not going to be the Ducati.

It wasn't. Aditya, for the first time ever since they had been dating, came for her in the metallic blue Mercedes convertible she had seen in his garage all that time ago. She stood by the car for a long moment, ogling it admiringly, then threw him a radiant smile. He had been staring at her, appreciating the very pretty picture she made, all blues, greens and silver, and smiled back at her, his heart in his eyes. They stood there for a moment till impatient honking behind them brought them back to earth.

'Wow, you managed to bring the car into the city's smallest lane,' she grinned even as she drank in the sight of him. He was in soft Madras checks today and the red, black and browns in the shirt suited him so well, decided his rather besotted girlfriend.

'Can I give you a kiss?' she asked him, suiting words to action before he could react, and planting a soft kiss on his cheek.

'You call that a kiss?' he asked with a glint in his eye.

'You don't?'

'No. I don't. Let me get you alone somewhere and I'll show you what a kiss is.'

'Promises, promises,' laughed Aditi but he was forced to let that go by, concentrating on negotiating the impossibly narrow, winding lane.

'Do you want the roof down?' he asked once they were on the bigger road and she immediately declined the offer.

'Can you imagine the state of my curls by the time we reach… where do we have to reach anyway?'

'Amma, Raj and Preetha live a stone's throw away from the Art of Living ashram on Kanakapura Road, quite near Mann's restaurant,' he told her. She digested that slowly. She ought to have known. She'd be meeting all of them. A whole lot of butterflies suddenly started moving inside her stomach.

She had calmed herself down by the time they got onto Kanakapura Road, though. She couldn't grudge him for wanting her to meet everyone at one go. And she wasn't going there as his future wife so there was nothing to worry on that score either, she figured. Just a visit, no big deal.

And then a sudden realization struck her. *He* was nervous. Not overtly so but there was a fine thread of tension in his lean body which she had only just cottoned onto.

Should she ask him why he was nervous, she wondered and then a rare vein of prudence prevailed and she held her tongue. 'What do you speak at home?' she asked him instead.

'Konkani but more of English. Just one of those things.'

'I know,' Aditi told him ruefully. 'Amma keeps telling us we must speak more often than we do in Malayalam. But somehow, we end up speaking more English than anything else.'

The house was redolent of a Bangalore long lost, a colonial

structure with a monkey-top roof, stone arches, two wings with turrets, a white-pillared portico, a large vine-wreathed trellis, and Aditi immediately fell in love with it. The building was painted a soft buttery cream, with the wooden slatted awnings above each window coloured a dark cinnamon brown. She could see a big closed terrace with a couple of stout stone pillars on both sides. Aditya parked under a mango tree and they walked towards the house in silence. The compound was a riot of colour. There were tabebuia trees in pink blossom, laburnums dripping yellow flowers, clusters of giant terracotta planters with beautiful plants in them, and beyond the main house she could spot a grove of mango trees. Aditya caught her look and said, 'There's an orchard out at the back. Mango, chickoo, guava, jackfruit, coconuts, all of it.' He smiled.

There was a large barn-like structure to one side of the house and a jacaranda poured its violet blossoms onto the roof with abandon.

No one seemed to be around to receive them. 'Do they know...' she began to ask and he nodded abruptly. Just as they reached the steps leading up to the house, the large doors panelled with coloured, frosted glass panes opened and Preetha stood there, smiling at them. She looked even more beautiful today, in a salwar-kurta block printed in the palest pink and green. Her large lustrous eyes shone with affection as they rested on her brother-in-law. He smiled and said casually, 'Hi, Preetha, all well?'

'You are late!' This was tempered with a smile to indicate she was joking. Aditi looked about with interest as Preetha led them through a front room into what was obviously the parlour. The floors were of red oxide and shone beautifully. The light fixtures were ornate, the curtains all had swags looped in a frill above them, marble-topped tables with enamel inlays stood here and there. The furniture was stately but comfortable. The house looked lived in.

The parlour was a symphony of soft pastel colours but Aditi had eyes only for the woman who rose from the long, low sofa as they came into the room. She had an oval face, large brown eyes and was smiling the sweetest smile. What took Aditi by surprise was that the face was young, unlined, the eyes tranquil and trouble-free. The snaps Aditi had seen online didn't do justice to the woman at all; if this was the woman Sudarshan Kamath had left, well he was an idiot!

Whoops, thought Aditi, suddenly. *What am I to address her as? Aunty? Mrs Kamath? Ms Shenoy? Amma?*

Aditya was already introducing her to his Amma. Aditi opted for an uncertain smile and stayed silent. She was conscious of her boyfriend watching her.

'What a lovely colour your skirt is, Aditi,' the older lady exclaimed with genuine delight. 'I had a sari just that colour years ago. Heaven knows where it is now.'

Putting her hand on Aditi's arm, she gently steered her to the sofa. 'You know Raj, don't you?' she asked and Aditi realized the other man was in the room.

He threw her a slightly sheepish smile but Aditi was having none of it. She had regained her characteristic aplomb by then. 'Hi Raj,' she said brightly, familiarly, for all the world as if she was meeting an old friend after a long time. Turning to his mother she said, 'We are practically old friends!'

That was audacious but it worked just as she knew it would. Amma was obviously in the know because she chuckled. Raj looked absolutely terror-stricken before recovering a bit and laughing weakly. Aditya was genuinely amused. As for Preetha, she threw Aditi an expressionless glance, then smiled. The younger girl was clearly meant to catch that look though.

Aditi looked Preetha squarely in the eye and her glance spoke volumes. It said, *I don't know what your problem is, lady, and I don't care. So get off my case, okay?*

Amma drew Aditi into conversation while the siblings and Preetha stood together, casually chatting. It was a large room, long-back wooden easy chairs and lovely little peg tables artfully arranged in corners. Aditi's eye caught the deep green glass lamp suspended above them. Following her glance, Amma laughed and said, 'I have inherited the house and everything in it from my parents. I am their only child.'

'It's lovely,' Aditi said politely but sincerely. She was trying her best to stay restrained and not come out sounding creepily intense about how much she loved the house at first sight.

'Yes but it's a nightmare to maintain,' Amma said lightly. 'We have a cook, her daughter does the top-work and her husband takes care of the compound and garden. What will you have to drink? Preetha does not believe in keeping any bottled drinks in the house, will you have some jal jeera?'

When she assented, Amma looked over at Preetha who immediately got up and left the room to get the drinks.

'How are things going, putha?' Amma asked Aditya, who came over to her, and loomed over her seated figure, smiling at both of them. Aditi felt warmed by the thought that he had included her in that smile.

'It's tough, Amma. The Canadians have a lot of conditions and are not too clued in on how things work here. Let's see how the next few weeks go.'

'Putha, I'm sure you will do whatever it takes to clinch the deal but do take care of yourself. Eat on time, sleep on time. It won't do to stress yourself out now, will it, Aditi?'

Caught by surprise, Aditi flashed both of them an uncertain smile. Though she had liked Aditya's smile of inclusion earlier, she was less than charmed at being included in this manner by Aditya's mother. But there was nothing she could do, so she said nothing. Then again, she thought reasonably, she had come here as his girlfriend so why was she shying away from being acknowledged as such?

Amma continued, 'I have tried my level best to teach my children to be self-sufficient. And they all are too, in many ways. But Aditya just won't cook, even on the days Radha can't go over and cook for him. And Raj can cook very well but after all these years, he still has not mastered the art of using the washing machine or doing the beds.'

Aditi had been covertly observing Raj. While on the surface everything seemed normal, he was clearly recovering from some ailment. Preetha had said something about recuperation. And on the heels of that thought, she remembered that Amma had been unwell too, and turned to ask her.

Amma caught the momentary hesitation as Aditi spoke and understood what it was about. 'My name is Shakunthala. You can call me Amma,' she said without any fuss.

'Amma, are you completely recovered from the dengue attack now?' she asked.

'Yes, yes, I'm okay. The doctor is an old friend and wanted me in the hospital for as long as he could have me there but I escaped! Apart from occasional bouts of tiredness, I'm doing fine.'

On cue, Aditya spoke up, saying solemnly, 'Eat on time, sleep on time. It won't do to stress yourself out now.' Amma made as if to slap his arm and he moved away chuckling.

Preetha came in with a rosewood tray filled with tall glasses, as Amma told Aditya, 'Raj is still not sleeping well, Adit. Maybe he needs a change in medication?'

Preetha came to an abrupt halt inside the doorway, throwing what Aditi interpreted as a frantic look at Aditya. Raj for his part, looked distinctly uncomfortable, as uncomfortable as Aditi was feeling. A faint crease appeared on Aditya's brow but when he spoke his voice was level.

'You need to visit the doc again, anna?' he asked and Raj moved convulsively, then muttered a 'No!'

Aditya turned to his Amma. 'It will take some time for Raj to fully recover, Amma. He needs rest. He'll be alright, I promise you.' Something in the way he said it seemed to reassure Amma and she fell silent.

Preetha relaxed then and brought over the drinks. She asked Aditi, 'How are things at work?'

'Things are going pretty well but I'm keeping my fingers crossed. A long good spell is usually followed by some crisis,' Aditi replied and that led Amma to enquire in detail about her line of work. 'Do you cook?' she asked the younger woman.

'She's a wonderful cook, actually,' Aditya said and Preetha immediately asked, 'Better than me? Better than Amma?'

Amma's face remained tranquil while both Aditya and Aditi looked uncomfortable. *Let him deal with it*, thought Aditi, then mentally doffed a hat to her boyfriend as he said smoothly, 'All three of you are wonderful cooks and I never cease to give thanks for it! I'm not sure Aditi can cook a soi bajjilli ghassi or a theeyal the way Amma and you do it, Preetha...but then, I'm not sure you guys can rustle up a Mallu theeyal the way she did at Onam time!'

He was disproved of the last at the lunch table when Amma and Aditi got into an intense discussion on just what went into the dishes served, and it became clear that Aditi Pillai knew her way around traditional Konkani cuisine too. Preetha looked a little disconcerted but quickly segued her way into the discussion. Lunch was a sumptuous spread consisting of dalitoy, the Konkani dal, kolambo, the traditional sambar, bhenda sagle which was coconut and bhindi, with pathrode, which was colocasia leaves stuffed with rice flour, along with stir-fried beans, sannas and rottis. As she ate, Aditi gazed about her. The tiles on the dining-room floor, she noticed, were a striking pattern in black and white. All the doorways had a stone trellis interlay at the top. This really was a stunning house.

'Did Preetha and you cook all this?' Aditi asked.

'Not everything,' Amma replied. 'Radha is our cook and she does the major work. She has been with us for many years now.'

Before she could stop herself, Aditi asked her boyfriend, 'Is this the same Radhamma who cooks for you?'

Amma laughed out loud, asking, 'Ah, she's been to your flat then, putha?'

To his credit, Aditya didn't turn a hair, saying, 'Yes, only once unfortunately. That's where Aditi met Preetha for the first time.'

Aditi looked across at the silent Raj and asked, 'How are things at Caboyea? I haven't drawn you as driver since the last time, though I take only Caboyea cabs now.'

Raj looked positively hunted, saying in a low voice, 'I haven't been to work for a while.'

'Oh yes, you've been ill,' Aditi said contritely and again caught some tension coming off both Raj's wife and brother. Only Amma seemed impervious. Aditi immediately turned the conversation onto something innocuous.

Dessert was coconut soufflé and garai, jackfruit payasam, something Aditi had had a lot of in its Malayali avatar. Amma was all for them to go back to the parlour and chat awhile but Aditya said in an apologetic tone, 'Sorry but I have a meeting later this evening, so is it okay if we leave now, Aditi?'

She nodded an immediate yes. Everyone came to the veranda to see them off. Preetha went over to Aditya and talked to him in a low tone, Raj stood in his characteristically awkward fashion almost wringing his hands and Amma turned to Aditi.

'I don't know if the two of you are serious about each other,' she said smiling sweetly. 'But I like you, Aditi, so do come again, with or without Aditya. We can talk food.'

They stood exchanging smiles and missed Aditya's pleased look from across the veranda.

The two of them drove away from the stately manor in a comfortable silence. The car moved like a dream even though the roads were pitted with ruts. They were still on moffusil roads with cane fields and big trees spreading their magnificent branches on both sides. Aditi mulled over something, then nodded to herself and asked him, 'When is your client meeting this evening?'

'Around sevenish…why?'

'Okay. Which means we have a little time.'

Aditya's eyes lit up. 'For what?' he asked teasingly, taking one hand off the steering wheel and caressing the side of her neck with the back of his fingers. Aditi quivered with delight but stayed focused.

'To talk,' she told him firmly. 'Remember, you did say we needed to talk, a while ago?'

He nodded and drove on till they came to a lovely raintree studded with gauzy pink flowers at this time of the year. He pulled up the car and switched off the ignition, turned to face her and said, 'Shoot.'

And she did. Beginning as was typical of her, with a question from left field. 'I heard you had a thing for bikes and owned a garage-full of them. Then how come you come for me on your Ducati all the time?'

Aditya looked at her for one startled second, then threw back his head and laughed. 'Wow! My girlfriend has Googled me! Actually, they got it wrong. My father loves bikes as much as I do. *He* has a collection of high-speed bikes. I have just my Ducati, not that I'm complaining.'

Which gave Aditi the opening she was looking for. 'Just what is your equation with your father, Aditya? If they live in that lovely old house, why does Raj drive a Caboyea car for a living, or is that what he really does for a living? Why does everyone treat him in such a fragile manner? And, if you are the younger son, how come you are Sudarshan Kamath's heir?'

She then took a deep breath and subsided, trying not to feel like she'd been too pushy. Dash it, they'd been dating for the better part of a full year now and it was time she got to know some things about him.

But Aditya looked into her bright eyes and smiled a smile full of understanding. There was something else there that she could not quite decipher.

'It's complicated,' he told her with a straight face. 'No, it really is. But let's start with Raj and here goes: Raj was made a junior partner in Caboyea but he likes to drive, he drives well and insists on driving a cab. My brother is a brilliant guy, he was a gold medallist at university. Then it all went downhill, at about the time my father's second marriage was going kaput, although there really isn't a connection.'

'Your father's *second* marriage?' she asked, a bit startled. 'He would have been more troubled when your father left your mother, na?'

'So one would imagine but Raj seemed to have it together at that time. He wasn't that young either, he had finished college by then,' he said. 'Then he started to hang with a really bad crowd and was soon into gambling, big-time. Started dropping serious money. More money than he could afford, than Amma could afford, than I could afford. When he fell in love with and married Preetha, he went clean, so to speak, for many years and we started to think the addiction was over. But…'

He took a deep breath, then went on. 'He's been in de-addiction centres twice and really does want to get off that wagon. He's putting Amma and Preetha—me too, if I'm honest—through hell but he just can't seem to help himself. Amma and I feel so bad about Preetha but she has coped very well all these years.'

Aditi slowly put two and two together. 'He just got out of a de-addiction centre?'

He shook his head sombrely. 'No, not rehab, this time he was in hospital. He had placed bets and lost a lot of money. When he refused to pay up, some bookies beat him up. We had a tough time keeping it out of the papers. I mean, Sudarshan Kamath's son and all that…'

'Your father disinherited Raj because of the gambling problem?' she asked huskily.

'Well, first Amma cut off all ties with my father when he married again. She said she could manage perfectly well without a paisa from him. Actually, to be fair to the man, he tried his best to make her see that bringing up two kids wasn't going to be easy without financial help. Amma's parents were landed gentry but no longer very wealthy.'

Aditi nodded. She had seen signs of shabby genteel chic here and there in the beautiful house, and had wondered about that.

'But Amma was adamant about her decision and Amma's a very determined woman. They eventually cut a deal. My father was going to see to the educational expenses of his sons and that was all. Amma would not, did not, take any money for herself from him.'

He turned to look straight ahead through the windshield. 'Why am I Sudarshan Kamath's sole heir? Well, my father is a determined man, too. He waited till I finished with university, then called me and told me he had made me his heir. He said he didn't think Raj would amount to much. And there you have it, this bloody messy situation.'

He suddenly hit the side of the steering wheel with a flat palm and the sound rang out like a gunshot. Aditi winced. But it was good, Aditya was slowly tearing down those walls he had built around himself.

He turned back to her and said slowly, 'But that damned situation is going to change. I wanted out of the whole mess years ago. I wanted to drop the Kamath surname and get out of my father's life. I managed the first and I'm in regular touch with the man only to rectify the situation.'

'Rectify it how?' Aditi asked, quite intrigued now.

'Well, he's ready to change his will, have both of us inherit even though not equally. It took some time and a lot of effort to get him to that point. His ego was hurt and though he's not the sort to bear grudges, his feelings of inadequacy always surface where Amma is concerned. Amma's the sticking point here and I'm working on that; sooner or later she'll have to see that she's unwittingly diddling Raj out of his father's rightful inheritance.'

'Hmmm,' Aditi said poring over the matter silently. It was complicated as he said, but she really admired him for taking the effort to put things right, as right as he could in these peculiar circumstances.

Aditya grinned suddenly. 'Now let me answer the questions you haven't asked yet,' he said.

'Like?' she asked back.

'Like, am I running Caboyea on Kamath money? Nope, it's seed money my partner and I have put in, with a couple of angel investors. Like, am I a mixed-up kid in desperate need of counselling? Nope, I think I worked out my demons a long time ago. Amma's loving but pragmatic care helped. Like, what's with the Kamath-Shenoy surname deal? That was my doing, I threw one helluva tantrum some years ago and took my mother's family surname.

'But you do realize this changes things, don't you?' he asked her, running a finger lightly over the outline of her lips. Aditi opened them to gently nibble at the finger. She didn't agree with his statement that he had worked out his demons. He was reticent, cautious, wary and they were all badges earned in a turbulent life, that much she knew now.

He said, 'Now that you know it all, I am left with just two choices.'

He moved closer and his mouth took over from his finger. They kissed passionately, her hand going up to caress his face, his fingers slipping into her neckline to caress the swell of her breast with a sure, firm touch.

She was breathless when they slowly moved apart.

'What are the two choices?' she asked, her voice all husky.

'I have to either kill you now that you know all my secrets.'

'Or?' she asked, anticipation mixed with dread inside her, because she knew what he would say next.

'Or I have to marry you to keep the secrets within the family.' He cocked an eyebrow, locking eyes with her.

She looked away hastily, desperately scrabbling around for something light and witty to say.

'Both those options sound drastic. There is a third choice,' she told him, as brightly as she could manage.

Clearly it wasn't what he was expecting her to say. He frowned. 'What?' he asked.

'I'll take the oath of Omerta. Secrecy above all else. I promise. Your secrets will be safe with me to the grave and beyond.'

He looked searchingly at her, started to say something but just then a tender-coconut seller tapped his side of the window.

'Saar! Meydum! Yelneer beka?' the man asked, and Aditya turned to her. She shook her head, he conveyed as much to the man and the moment was thankfully past.

They drove away in another kind of silence, a thoughtful one. He had a habit of resting his hand lightly on his thigh while driving, then moving it fluidly to change gears, and she stared at it hypnotized.

She had some veggie-buying to do, so she asked him to drop her off at the head of Tippasandra's main road. Just as she got out, he said, 'Aditi.'

She turned to look at him.

'We need to talk some more,' he told her, then stroked her cheek and raised his hand in salute.

CHAPTER TEN

Aditi lost no sleep over the inevitable confrontation that was now staring her in the face. As she had told Ritu, she would cross that bridge when she came to it.

Funnily enough, when she woke up it was not with Aditya on her mind but an idea for the Snack Team.

'Olives?' asked Raman in a distinctly doubtful manner. Mickey kept a tactful silence while Pia's expression mirrored Raman's.

Aditi was undaunted. 'Yes,' she exclaimed brightly. 'Snacks, all of them featuring olives in one form or another. A relish, a paté, a spread for open sandwiches…oh, you get the idea, don't you?'

Raman scratched the side of his nose. 'Yes, but you do know that olives really haven't taken off big in India? And it kind of shifts our "local food first" goalpost, doesn't it?'

Aditi replied, 'Well, we also experiment with bringing new foods to the customer, don't we? Let's give it a shot? Here's how I see the plan. We get our snack-makers to go for bust with new ideas, new tastes featuring the not-so-humble olive, then we market it to potential clients. Once we are over the initial mindset hurdle, once the novelty factor appeals, once the taste kicks in and catches on, watch how it clicks.'

Support came from an unexpected source. 'Hey, Boss Lady, I think that's a rad idea!' said Bobby, who was lurking in a corner of the room unnoticed till then.

'Rad? Oh surely not rad,' said Mickey trying hard to stifle a grin.

But Bobby, like Aditi earlier, remained undaunted. 'It *is* rad!' he insisted. 'We buy bottled olives to have as snacks with our drinks, don't we? Now let's put olives on bread and biscuit bases and watch people go for it!'

The four seniors exchanged looks. Mickey took the call. 'Okay, let's go for it. But let's do a small numbers test first. If our chefs can rustle up something good, then we are on a roll. If not, we'll cut our losses immediately.'

'Thank you, Aditi,' she told the room at large with a straight face. Everyone stared at her for a moment, and she stared back, asking, 'What? I don't deserve thanks?' Raman and Mickey laughed even as Pia asked plaintively, 'Why are you thanking yourself, Aditi?'

However, after that one show of support, Bobby alas, went back to form. Either it was a bad day for him or for his office colleagues. He dropped a folder stacked with loose but very important papers, then tore a couple of those papers as he was trying to pick them up and put them back in place. He took a client call and remembered to note the message down but forgot to note the client's name. He offered to go on a follow-up visit to one of their supply kitchens but came back indoors in a minute saying his bike had a flat tyre. When he asked to go home early ('Gotta take my girl out,' he said), they assured him that it was perfectly okay to depart forthwith.

'Take a Caboyea since your bike's bust,' offered Aditi as parting advice but Bobby was out of the door so fast, she doubted he had heard her.

'How can we let our interns get away like this?' Pia asked in a troubled manner. 'He didn't even have a good excuse. He said he wanted to go home early to take his girlfriend out!'

'At least he was honest, Pia,' Raman said. 'Let's celebrate that honesty.'

Pia and Raman had started going out but were keeping it very casual, as of now. The odd movie or dinner was what they averaged, once a week.

'Raman is quite sweet actually,' Pia confided in Aditi.

'Not so much an uncle?' teased Aditi but Pia had forgotten her earlier comment about Raman.

'Whose uncle?' she asked, quite baffled. 'He's an only kid. I don't think he has nieces and nephews.'

Aditi had to quickly drop that line of teasing. Experience had taught her that it was better to quit when ahead than enter a labyrinth of explanations and clarifications with the slightly woolly-headed Pia.

Aditi spent most of her time after work these days with the anti-flyover committee which consisted of architects, city planners, activists and Bangaloreans who knew just what it was that they wanted and did not want. They were streamlining preparations for the upcoming silent protest. As a noted veteran journalist had written recently in his monograph on Bangalore, the citizens accepted that the plundering class needed no reasons for plundering, they only needed pretexts. And the activists were trying to reduce those pretexts by partnering with government agencies, even if the going was indeed very tough for them.

And so it was that she did not meet her boyfriend all that busy week, though they texted each other many times a day and spoke on the phone every night. Friday morning, she received a message that asked: **Dinner at my place?**

As it happened, Aditi and Pia had made plans to go catch a movie and then try out a new Japanese place down the road from the miniplex. Aditi wasn't going to bail out on her girlfriend for her boyfriend but she didn't have to because Pia came up to her cubicle in the early afternoon and asked, 'Can I give you haath for this evening's programme?'

Aditi laughed at the use of a term she had not heard for a while now.

'Sure, you can give me haath,' she told the other girl. 'Wassup?'

'Well, Raman and I want to sign up for spoken Kannada classes. We thought we'd go check the place out...'

'Oh, okay, sounds good,' Aditi said and immediately sent her boyfriend a text saying **It's on!**

Pick you up around 8 on the bike, came the reply.

Aditya, she knew from experience, was nothing if not punctual, so a few minutes before eight she was ready and waiting, clad in skintight jeans shredded to alarming and definitely provocative levels, paired with a navy blue and red shirt, under which she wore a deep-blue cami. On impulse, she washed her hair, dried it out after applying industrial-strength conditioner and left it loose, with a scrunchie on her wrist to hold it while she was on the bike. Her regulation silverware caught the light and glinted most alluringly.

At eight sharp he was there at her door, one helmet tucked under his arm, the other hanging by its strap from his hand.

She smiled and said chirpily, 'Let's go!'

'Not yet,' he murmured and gently walked her backwards into the flat, kicking the front door shut with the heel of his boot. Then he proceeded to kiss her, slowly and thoroughly, in the most delicious fashion. Her face was flushed when he finally lifted his head.

'Can I come out now?' asked a voice from the dining room and they turned to see Ritu there, one eyebrow raised in mockery.

'Oh don't let us stop you, it's your house,' Aditya told her suavely. Both girls started to giggle.

'No but really, guys. If you are going to start getting hot and heavy, do it in the privacy of a closed room, not in the living room!'

Aditi inclined her head graciously. 'Thank you for that piece of sound advice, Aunty,' she said demurely.

'Where are we going?' she asked Aditya when he had wheeled his way carefully out of the minuscule lanes of Tippasandra, which as always was crammed with cars, two-wheelers, burly buses and a million pedestrians all at once. She looped her arms around his waist and let her helmeted head rest lightly on his back.

'My place?' he said in reply, the lilt to his words acting like a question.

'Okay,' she said then added, 'but let's go for a long ride first.'

And it was a pleasurable long ride once they left Bangalore's eternally gridlocked traffic behind. The road wasn't very good but he nimbly avoided all the crater-like potholes, giving the bike full throttle when he could. She raised her face to feel the wind on it; she loved this bike, she loved the man riding the bike, she loved life. Aditi felt little bursts of joy exploding inside her.

Radhamma had cooked Chinese food for them and it was very good Chinese, too. There was stir-fried chicken in black-bean sauce, the ubiquitous gobi Manchurian which Aditi was crazy about, there was rack of lamb basted in a spicy garlic sauce, and loads of fig stewed in ginger sauce for dessert. Radhamma for sure was one amazing cook.

They ate quietly and comfortably, catching up with each other's work-week, making plans to watch a play at Ranga Shankara next week, pausing to smile into each other's eyes often.

Replete at last, she pushed her plate away and said, 'How on earth do you manage to keep so trim with this kind of heavenly home-cooked food?'

He just grinned in reply. And she knew the answer; Aditya's metabolism was clearly an inherited one. Both Sudarshan Kamath and Shakunthala Shenoy were people without an extra ounce of fat on them.

'Coffee? A shot of liquer?' he asked and she shook her head, suddenly feeling a little awkward.

Quickly launching into speech, she asked, 'Shall we clear up?' They cleared the table and stacked the dishes into the dishwasher in a matter of minutes.

'Wanna catch the news?' he asked. A cyclone had hit the neighbouring states and both of them had friends in Chennai and Hyderabad. They watched with a sense of relief as the news anchor reported that the cyclone had made landfall and was now in the process of moving on.

They sat on the large couch, Aditya's arm around her shoulders. After a while, his hands started to caress the nape of her neck, just under her thick curls. As the reporter prattled on about other inconsequential matters, he slowly, deliberately turned and looked into her eyes. She stared steadily back. He ran a warm questing finger on the expanse of bare skin revealed by the strategic rips on her jeans and she blindly turned her face into his neck, nuzzling his collarbone, then planting a series of feather-light kisses on his jaw.

Their mouths met with explosive hunger and they kissed hard and hungrily. She wound her arms around his neck, caressing the back of his head. He raised the hem of her shirt and slipped his hand inside, to cup and caress a breast. Her nipples sprang to life and she gave a small moan.

Then he drew away and told her huskily, 'Let's go upstairs, to my bedroom?'

Aditi didn't do coy at the best of times and she wasn't going to do so now. 'Okay,' she agreed and he dropped a soft kiss on her temple.

She was seeing his bedroom for the first time. Done up in cream and browns, it had a male sparseness, a minimalist look that she found quite appealing. There was a large sepia photograph of a beautiful building above the bed.

She stood in the middle of the room not knowing what to do next, then Aditya was beside her, taking her into his arms. There was just one lamp on, beside the bed, and it cast a soft, muted light in the room.

Mouth still locked on hers, he gently walked her to the bedside and in one swift smooth motion swept her off her feet and onto the bed, landing lightly beside her. He began to trail kisses on the length of her neck and she gave a small moan of delight. Before she knew it, her shirt was off. Pushing the neckline of her cami aside, he started to kiss the swell of her breasts, then told her firmly, 'We need to get these off you.'

In for a penny, in for a pound, Aditi told herself and sat up, pulling her camisole over her head. He watched her intently, a glitter in his dark eyes. She sat back on her knees, preparing to remove her jeans and then he moved, planting open-mouthed kisses on all the places where her skin showed. Slowly, steadily, he unbuttoned her jeans, then pulled down the zip.

'It's really and truly skintight. It's not going to come off that easily,' she said on the ghost of a laugh.

'Let me try,' he replied, gently tumbling her back onto the bed. She raised her bottom all the better to get the jeans moving down her legs, and within seconds, Aditya had them off her and was lightly flinging them to one side.

He stared at her as she lay there, her hair a halo of spirals on his pillow, her figure clad only in a very fetching pair of deep pink bra and panties.

'This,' he told her with satisfaction, 'is how I have pictured you a million times. Here on my bed, just this way…'

Lowering himself beside her, he started to nuzzle her breasts, not removing her bra. Gently he licked the soft lace at the spot where her nipple was and it sprang to life under his tongue.

'That's so…so…so amazing,' she moaned.

Now his expert fingers were smoothly divesting her of both bra and panties, and she suddenly realized he still had his clothes on. That too was sexy, very sexy. However, he had to get out of those clothes if things were to move along, she decided.

'We need to get these off you,' she told him in the exact matter-of-fact tone he had used on her. Their eyes met and he chuckled, then she got busy. Slowly, taking her own time, she unbuttoned and slipped his linen shirt off him, dropping light kisses on his shoulders, along his collarbone, all the while. Then her fingers went to work on his jeans which proved as hard to remove as hers had been.

'Let me do that,' he told her huskily, suiting action to word. He wore briefs not boxers, she registered in some dim part of her brain and watched through half-closed eyes as both jeans and jocks went the way of her clothes onto the carpet by the bed.

She continued to survey him through half-closed eyes in a dreamy fashion, taking in his ripped torso, slim waist, hair-roughened, muscled legs.

And then he was above her, looming for an instant before he brought his body down lithely onto hers. She stiffened for a minute but was too caught up in the moment to be nervous. He was doing wonderful things and she found she couldn't think. He kissed her breasts, lightly taking the nipples into his mouth and sucking on them till she moaned. Then he started to weave his way down her body, leaving kisses as he went, on her cleavage, her belly button, down to where she was wet and pulsing for him. As he moved his mouth on her, she went quietly, gloriously mad.

Then he was sliding back up over her body to find her mouth urgently, hungrily. They kissed fervently, passionately and he was looming over her again, straddling her slim body before slowly entering her. This time her body went stiff in an unmistakable fashion and Aditya paused in the act. He looked down into her eyes. What she saw in his eyes was enough to calm her down; she slowly and deliberately relaxed her body, lifted her legs and crossed them behind his back. The movement brought her even closer to him and this time it was Aditya who groaned.

He thrust slowly, very slowly, into her and soon, she had caught the rhythm too, moving to meet it. They made hard and fast love after Aditi's initial hesitation, and they climaxed together in one glorious moment.

As they lay there, Aditi's head in the crook of his shoulder, waiting for their heartbeats to return to normal, she turned her face up to him and said in her usual direct way, 'That was mind-blowing.' Then she added softly, 'I'm not the most experienced of women, y'know.'

He looked at her and smiled a wry smile. 'I know. I cottoned on quite some time ago. That's why I did not want to rush into things.'

'Fuck!' she said, reaching up to kiss his jawline. 'But how did you know?'

He grinned. 'I could say I just did. But there were many giveaway signs.'

Now she was intrigued. 'Such as?' she asked, one hand lightly caressing his chest hair absentmindedly.

'You weren't really walking your talk,' he told her. 'And your talk was that of a woman of the world. One who has seen it all, done it all. Then, there's the look in your eyes...'

'Not Little Miss Innocence!' she protested, pulling at his chest hair.

'Ouch,' he said. 'Actually, yes. Even when you were cursing, using language your mother would be shocked to know you know. Even as you were throwing back tequila shots.'

'Ouch,' she said, mimicking him. 'Now you are making me out to be some kind of fake type who is attempting to up my cool quotient.' She felt both annoyed and chagrined that he had seen through her act but most of all, she felt a little embarrassed. As always, she used humour to fight her way out.

He turned to face her, propping his head on his hand. 'A fake? Not for a minute,' he told her lovingly, so lovingly, Aditi felt a lump come into her throat. 'You were just waiting for me to come along. Right?'

The one-word question was asked seriously. She looked him in the eye and sighed happily. 'Yes, my darling,' she told him. 'Now kiss me.'

He bent his head down obediently and soon, they were aflame, which led to another most satisfactory interlude.

Aditi woke to the sun shining directly into her eyes; rays of sunlight were coming through the gaps in the curtains. She also woke to her boyfriend's exploratory hands. They were spooning together and his body warmth was doing things to her, the best kind of things.

'Mmm,' she exclaimed on a note of sheer pleasure. 'Don't stop...'

'I wasn't going to', he assured her, as he pulled her body closer to his. Then he said, 'But first...'

Gently flipping her onto her back, he looked into her eyes and said, 'I love you.' Simply and starkly, his eyes burning into hers.

Aditi shut her eyes for a quick moment, then opened them, delight blazing out of them.

'Darling Aditya,' she told him, caressing his shoulder, 'I love you too.'

They sealed their declaration with a kiss, this time a kiss of love declared, love acknowledged.

Then she reverted to type. 'I'm hungry,' she told him.

'So am I,' he growled, reaching for her but she staved him off.

'No, I mean I'm hungry for food!'

He stilled, then chuckled. 'Okay, let me go check what's in the fridge.'

A sudden thought struck her. 'Omigawd!' she exclaimed in horror. 'Will Radhamma be in the kitchen?'

'No, she comes in late in the mornings,' he said, then added, 'but why should that bother you?'

Aditi eyed him warily. 'Why should that not bother me?' she queried.

He looked confused for a moment. Then carefully picking his words, he said, 'I meant, she will have to get used to seeing you here.'

'Why?' she further demanded of him. 'Are you about to ask me to move in with you?'

He had been pulling on his clothes but now stopped, going still for a moment. Then shirt still unbuttoned, he came up to the bed and smiled down at her, his heart in his eyes.

'No,' he told her quite firmly. 'I am not going to ask you to move in with me.'

She exhaled, then told him quite chattily, 'Oh good. Because I'd have had to say no. I like my Tippy flat and what would Rits do if I walked out on her; also…'

He bent down and laid one long finger on her mouth. 'Listen up for a minute, won't you?' he asked. Then he continued, 'Because I am about to propose.'

Aditi couldn't breathe for a whole moment. 'P…p…propose,' she stuttered. 'Propose what?'

'Well, I'm not going to make you any kind of indecent proposition, Aditi Pillai. I'm not that kind of guy, and you know that.' He was grinning that endearing grin of his, wholly expecting her to share in the joke. Only, she couldn't.

She closed her eyes again. Oh, she'd known this moment lay in wait, just around the corner, but she had also been hoping she wouldn't have to turn that corner for some time yet.

She swallowed, then opened her eyes to find him looking down at her with a crease between his brows. 'What is it, darling?' he asked her gently and she nearly cried.

But she had to get it out. 'Don't,' she murmured, closing her eyes in defence. 'Just don't.'

The silence that filled the room after she said that was so heavy, it almost choked her.

'Don't ask you to marry me, Aditi?'

Eyes still squeezed shut like a small child, she nodded.

'But why? Am I rushing things? Is that it? Do you want some time to think things over?'

When she looked at him, he lowered himself onto the bed and ran a hand softly over her cheek. 'I thought we have a good thing going…am I wrong? Isn't it time we took things to the next level?'

At that, she found her voice. 'We just did,' she told him, forcing herself to look directly at him.

He smiled but there was concern lurking in his face. Whatever he had expected, it was clearly not this. And he knew that she wasn't a tease, so he was trying his hardest to suss the situation out.

'Aditi Pillai, you are the love of my life,' he told her, his face serious, his eyes smiling. 'I want to marry you, have kids with you, live a life of love, laughter, some squabbling, much making up, all with you. I have waited a long time to meet a girl like you. Now that I have found you, I want to make things permanent. Isn't that what you want too?'

She shook her head and he looked poleaxed. Then she launched into breathless speech. 'Oh, I love you too, Aditya. You are the best thing that has happened to me. And I do want to be with you forever and ever. But I don't believe in marriage...I don't want to get married.'

She thought he would spring off the bed in anger but he only continued to caress her face.

'Why, darling?' he asked her. 'Tell me. Have you been scarred by a break-up in your life, a break-up in the life of someone close to you?'

She side-stepped that and said, real despair in her voice. 'I could tell you it's like how some people are petrified of dogs without ever having kept one. But that will sound facile, and I can't be facile about this.' She stopped talking abruptly but he gestured for her to continue.

'It's just that I think marriage is a one-sided proposition and it is totally in favour of men. They get someone in their bed, someone to keep their house looking like something out of a woman's magazine, they get someone to see to their food, their laundry, manage their investments and bear children for them. Oh, and throw the most amazing parties, too.

'No, don't tell me you have a cook, an investment consultant, a laundry service that picks up your clothes three times a week, maybe a party planner too...'

'I do,' he interjected with a smile that didn't quite reach his eyes.

'But that's not the point I'm making Aditya, and I'm sure you get that. What I have seen is that it's the woman who gets the lopsided end of this bargain. She has to move house, learn to juggle a hundred responsibilities, she has to run her household while finishing work deadlines and she gets stuck with the blame if the party falls flat, the food is inedible, the work projects fall through, the children fall ill, if love goes flying out of the window, whatever...'

Now he looked thoughtful. 'These are things modern couples work on, they are not insurmountable problems. And love doesn't always go flying out of the window.'

Then he leaned forward to look intently into her eyes. 'How about a long engagement? To ease you into things?'

But she had begun shaking her head before he ended his sentence and he sat back in resignation. 'I really hadn't thought you were such a cynic, Aditi,' he said, almost conversationally.

'I'm not!' she protested. 'I'm just being practical.' Then she sat up on her knees in bed, hurriedly wrapping the snowy white linen sheet around her. Reaching out a hand to him pleadingly, she said, 'I really really really love you. I want to be with you all my life. But marriage will change the nature of our feelings for each other.'

He looked at her impassively. 'What are you suggesting? That we meet to hook up twice a week? Or given our work schedules, maybe every weekend?'

The tone was frosty. 'Aditya?' she asked uncertainly.

The atmosphere had changed abruptly, she could sense it. He continued to look at her but she could see the imperceptible hardening of the expression on his face. He took a deep breath, then said, 'Okay. I've got to tell it like it is. I am very disappointed, Aditi. I offered you my love, I offered you the rest of my life for us to live together, share our joys and sorrows, enjoy each other's company. And you threw it back in my face.'

She opened her mouth to speak, looked at his face and shut up. Aditya was not done yet. 'The thing is, I'm an old-fashioned kind of guy. Marriage means a lot to me, I don't, I won't, take it lightly. I've seen what happens if you take it lightly, remember?

'So,' he continued. 'The way I see it, you don't love me enough to want to live with me for the rest of our lives. Fair enough. But I don't do casual…'

Here she cut in rashly, a little desperately. 'I could move in here with you, Aditya?'

He gave a short laugh and she winced at the sound of it. 'Shouldn't you wait until you are asked?' he asked her, the tone gentle, his eyes fierce.

In despair, she wailed, 'Aditya, don't be like this!'

'Like what?' he asked implacably. Then he rose from the bed and turned to leave the room. Before he moved, he asked her in all politeness, 'What will you have for breakfast?'

She wanted to say 'Nothing' and run off home as fast as she could. But that was the coward's way and Aditi was no coward. 'Whatever you find in the fridge,' she told him in a subdued tone.

Breakfast was sheer hell for her and he didn't look too comfortable either. It took on the air of a test, so they sat at the table and ate their fried eggs and buttered toast in a tense, fraught silence. She looked at him several times as he sat with his back to the sun streaming in through the windows. He met her eyes without flinching but the barrier he had erected was a very tangible one and she just did not know how to breach it.

'I'll drop you home,' he told her but she declined and he did not press the matter. At the door, she turned and asked him, 'Are we saying bye for good, Aditya?'

'I don't know,' he told her politely, that distant look still on his face. 'Are we?'

She threw caution to the winds then. 'No!' she told him fiercely. 'I won't let you go out of my life.' She leaned forward to kiss him but he stepped back and said, 'Then marry me.' Now there was nothing cold or aloof about his tone; on the contrary, he was pleading with her.

'I can't!' she cried. 'I'd be shortchanging you, shortchanging myself!'

The distant look returned, touched with bleakness. 'If that's the way you see it,' he said with a shrug.

When Aditi walked in the door, Ritu was doing yoga in the living room. She sat up, took in Aditi's stony face and stormy eyes and rushed to envelop her in a bear-hug.

'Oh Addy!' she exclaimed. 'What happened?'

Aditi couldn't trust herself to speak, she needed to sort out the million thoughts buzzing in her brain, and she wanted the privacy of her bedroom to do that. So she shook her head and managed to whisper, 'Later.' Then she rushed into her room, where she threw herself onto the bed and gave in to a short burst of angry tears. She cried for her inability to cross this terrible commitment hurdle; she cried for Aditya's intractability and unwillingness to see things her way; she cried for what had been a wonderful relationship with the one man she had actually fallen in love with.

And after that bout of tears, she sat up filled with fresh anger. What the bloody hell! Had she just been dumped? Just because she had clear-cut ideas about marriage? Surely Aditya wasn't just another guy who wanted things to always go his way? If he was, then he didn't deserve her. And if he wasn't, it was just going to be a matter of time before he came to his senses.

On the heels of this optimistic thought, she reached for her box of tissues and blew her nose noisily, just as Ritu walked in with a huge cup of something.

'Enough moping,' Ritu declared cheerfully, her eyes giving away her concern though. 'Drink up this jasmine tea and you'll feel heaps better.'

Aditi obediently took the cup and started to sip from it. She was feeling drained now.

She looked up and caught Ritu's eye. Then she took a deep breath and baldly announced, 'Aditya proposed to me. And I said no.'

Ritu closed her eyes, then opened them again. 'Of course you did,' she exclaimed softly but without any accusation in her voice. 'And he took it bad.'

'Big-time bad,' Aditi agreed. 'But he's not rid of me, no way. I just need time to get him to see things my way.'

'And how do things look your way?' Ritu asked. Aditi glared at her. 'No, I'm not trying to provoke you, Addy. I really want to know...'

This time Aditi chose her words with care. 'I have to get him to see that if a relationship is rock-solid, which I think ours is, then we don't need the sanction of a piece of paper to give it respectability. I want a long-term, committed relationship. Just not marriage.'

'So you will move in with him?'

'If he wants me to,' she replied. Just talking her way through this thicket was helping her.

'Oh-kay,' Ritu said thoughtfully. 'Now help me figure this out. Are you sure you are not flying the banner of no-marriage just for the heck of it, Addy? Misplaced sense of ego and all that?'

'No!' she replied angrily. 'I'm not that stupid! It's just that I really don't believe in the institution of marriage, not the way it is today.' Counting off on her fingers, she said, 'Basically, marriage is all about legalized sex, financial security, physical security, the propagation of one's line through children. I don't need legalized sex, thank you. I'm earning well, I can take care of myself, I'm not eyeing Aditya Shenoy's wealth and something tells me he's not eyeing mine, either! As for kids, I haven't given that any kind of thought…'

Ritu sighed. 'But what about your parents? You know they are hoping you will grow out of this phase? Your mother used the phrase "grow up," actually.'

There was a stubborn tilt to Aditi's chin. 'I guess they will just have to accept that this is not a temporary phase in their daughter's life, it is a belief she holds dear. A belief she has held dear for many years now.' The chin went up further as she asked Ritu, 'You think I'm being stupid?'

'Not for a minute. I'm mostly on the same commitment-phobic side as you, remember? I just hope Aditya gets his priorities right.' Saying this, she leaned forward to give Aditi a quick hug.

'What about work? Going in today?'

Aditi nodded. She wasn't going to let her personal affairs come in the way of work. She'd never done so and wasn't about to start now.

CHAPTER ELEVEN

It was a lacklustre day at the office. Aditi went over some paperwork with Pia and Raman, then made some phone calls, and that was it. This was not good because she needed something to occupy herself with or else she'd start to brood. Mickey was out on a work call. Bobby was even more skittish than usual today and Aditi eyed him thoughtfully. She noticed Anita was covering up for him virtually all the time these days. What was the matter with the boy? Was he some kind of pothead?

Cornering both of them near the coffee-maker, she asked in a kindly tone, 'So. You guys liking your internship here?'

Both of them chorused a quick yes. 'I'm learning so much!' Anita said, adding, 'I think I'm going to make food my future career.'

'Good show,' Aditi told her, then turned to the silent young man. 'What about you, Bobby?'

'I don't know what I'm going to be doing in the future,' he replied nonchalantly. 'I believe in living for the day.'

'Hmmm,' Aditi said. 'Not a bad way to live.' Bobby threw a searching glance at her, then relaxed when he understood that she wasn't being judgmental. 'The thing is,' he confided, 'I want to play in a band. But my parents won't hear of it.'

Aditi was a bit startled at this sudden confession but she kept her smile. 'What instrument do you play? Or do you sing?'

'I sing and I play the guitar,' he told her proudly. Anita put in excitedly, 'He totally slays it!'

Aditi threw her a thoughtful look. Was she dating Bobby? She could do better…

'Well, all the best and I hope you get to realize your dreams, Bobby but in the meantime, you need to be pulling your weight here, okay?'

The day wore on endlessly. She kept checking her phone for messages but there was nothing from Aditya. Pia and she went down the road to their regular ramen place where Pia brought Aditi up-to-date on her romance. All was going very well, it seemed.

'Whoever knew!' Pia marvelled and Aditi grinned.

'Of course we knew! We knew Raman had feelings for you, as they say in Hollywood films! It was only you who went around with blinkers on.'

Pia then asked what Aditi was hoping she wouldn't. 'What about you and the F1 driver, Addy?'

'What about us?' she asked, stalling for time.

'You two seem serious. Getting engaged or something?'

'Nope,' she replied shortly. 'All's cool as it is.' She loved Pia but she just didn't have the energy to discuss Aditya with the other girl right now.

She decided to take off from work early but Mickey walked in just as she picked up her bag to leave.

'Hey, where are you going? I gotta tell you guys about the olive chase.'

Raman, Pia and Aditi looked enquiringly at him with varying degrees of interest.

'Two clients agreed to give it a shot but made it clear all

liabilities would be ours to bear. The third refused outright. The fourth said they were in if we replaced olives with something more popular like tomato. Or potato. Or paneer.'

The next half-hour went in discussing just what they had going and how they could take it forward. Given that this had been her idea, Aditi now gave it full focus. Typically though, all the Snack Team members were now wholeheartedly into the olive project whether they agreed with Aditi or not. It was one of the reasons she loved this bunch.

As the meeting broke up and they returned to their cubicles, Mickey said, 'Aditi?'

She turned to find him looking at her with a small crease between his eyebrows.

'What?' she asked.

'All okay? You look a bit off.'

She had never lied to him and she wouldn't now. She threw him a speaking glance and Mickey drew a sharp breath.

'Are you going home?' he asked and she nodded. 'Okay, I'll be along soonest I finish some pending stuff here.'

True to his word, he was there soon enough, plonking himself on the yak-skin rug while she made him a cup of tea.

'Tell me all,' he told her, when she had brought him the tea and seated herself beside him.

'Aditya proposed marriage. I turned him down. He's mad as hell. I'm upset as hell. Finito,' she said, trying for a nonchalant tone and failing miserably.

Mickey took it literally and asked, 'Finito? You mean he and you are over?'

'No!' Then she took a deep breath and said, 'No. At least, I hope not. But we are not in a happy place right now.'

Mickey didn't say anything. She gave him a pleading look and said, 'I could do with the male perspective here, Micks. Did I do wrong in turning him down?'

'Well, you hit him—hard—where it hurts him the most, his pride. No guy proposes easily, at the drop of a hat, least of all a reserved kind of man like your boyfriend. But then you've always said you don't believe in marriage, for so many years now. So I am sure you weren't stringing Aditya on.'

Tentatively, she asked, 'Why is it so important for him to marry me?'

Mickey gave her a wry look. 'Don't be daft, Addy. Given his less-than-calm background, the guy's looking to settle down in every sense of the word. It's more than marriage. It's a home, a place where he can take off all his masks, it's a partner who will stand by him like a rock. Unlike his father.'

Aditi burst out, 'I will! I will stand by him like a rock.'

Mickey shook his head sadly. 'He wants the comfort offered by that piece of paper. The very piece of paper you flee like a bat out of hell from.'

'But you understand my point of view, don't you?'

He gave her a lopsided smile. 'I do. I'm not in your headspace but I do. You are a free spirit and you feel marriage will clip your wings…'

'It's more than that, Micks. I feel it will burden me with all sorts of responsibilities. And it always works in the most deceptive ways. You enter into it thinking you can tackle it, then it takes you down. You struggle and realize everyone expects you to succeed, cutting you absolutely no slack.'

Now Mickey reacted with some asperity. 'Don't be a fool,' he admonished her. 'Which century are you still living in? These are things a couple sits down and sorts out before they get married…'

'Oh, really?' she challenged him. 'Did you and Minu sit down and discuss money, children and your old girlfriends before you took the saat pheras?'

He looked taken aback, then shrugged. 'No but ours was an arranged marriage, remember?'

She sighed in exasperation because she really didn't see why an arranged marriage did not need a pre-marital talk, then tried a different tack. 'Okay. Name one couple you know, we know, who have sat and discussed all this before getting hitched…?'

Mickey fell silent, the wheels in his head turning. Aditi waited patiently. Then he shook his head. 'Actually, I don't know anyone who had this kind of talk before tying the knot. Which is something most of them should have done, the fools. I hear Shekhar and Priya are seeing a marriage counsellor…'

Aditi allowed herself to be temporarily diverted. But as Mickey was leaving, he turned to her and asked seriously, 'Shall I go meet Aditya?'

She gave him a quick hug and said warmly, 'No thanks, Micks. We'll work this out ourselves. If we are meant to be together, then better sense will prevail…'

Mickey laughed low in his throat and said gruffly, 'I won't bother asking whose better sense.'

Aditi then embarked on Operation Stalk Boyfriend. She sent Aditya messages every night, warm and loving messages, cheeky messages, suggestive messages, naughty messages. The number of messages decreased every night as they met with absolutely no response. She checked his Twitter handle, his Facebook page, his Snapchat account. His relationship status on Facebook remained reassuringly unchanged but he clearly was not going on any of those social platforms too often.

Where the bloody hell was he? What was he doing?

On the fourth evening, she caved in and called him. The phone rang several times and she was about to click off when she heard his voice, so familiar, so beloved.

'Hi, Aditi,' he said most amicably.

'Hi, sweetie,' she said, her words rushing into each other in her relief that she was at last touching base with him. 'How are you doing? You...'

He cut in, 'I'm sorry I haven't been able to revert. I'm not in Bangalore, I'm travelling.'

She immediately registered the cautious choice of words and was hurt. What, now he wasn't going to tell her where he was? Well, she *was* going to ask.

'Where are you?'

'I'm in Mumbai, flying out to Vancouver tomorrow.'

The silence stretched between them. 'And when will you be back?' she asked, throwing pride to the winds.

There was a momentary hesitation on his part. 'I'm not sure. I'll call you when I'm back in town.'

'Aditya?' she asked, her voice throbbing with emotion but he quickly said, 'Gotta go, Aditi. Take care.'

'Hey, a man's gotta work when he's gotta work,' Ritu told her in a falsely hearty tone later that night. 'You did say he was in talks to tie up with a Canadian firm, didn't you?'

Aditi nodded forlornly. 'Oh, it's not that he's away. It's the polite, distant way he spoke to me...he's gone back into his aloof shell.'

'Well, what do you expect, Addy?' Ritu asked gently. 'You've dealt him a blow and men take time to recover from blows dealt by women...'

Aditi stared at her friend. 'And women?' she demanded.

'And women what?' the other girl asked, looking baffled.

'What do women do to recover from blows to the heart?'

Ritu stared back at her. She nibbled the tip of her finger and thought for a moment. Then she said, 'Women go out and get drunk. We are women. We need to recover. So: shall we?'

Aditi thought that was a dashed good idea and soon the girls were at their favourite pub all the way over in Whitefield, ordering G and Ts at a rapid clip, raising toast after toast to a speedy recovery. It didn't take long for the two of them to feel warm and fuzzy.

'Why are you drinking?' Aditi asked Ritu with a mischievous look in her eyes. 'What do you need to recover from?'

'I'm drinking to drown your sorrows,' Ritu told her primly, reaching for her glass and clutching it like it was a goblet of gold. 'Adulting,' she further pronounced, for all the world as if she was just emerging from her teens, 'is so bloody hard.' Aditi nodded her head vigorously.

'So right you are,' she told Ritu, approvingly. Then she was struck by a sudden thought. 'Even if we have to walk back to town, we are not taking a Caboyea car home, okay?'

'Okay,' Ritu agreed affably, if vaguely.

Aditi wasn't done yet. 'We are never going to take a Caboyea cab. Ever.'

Now Ritu looked disconcerted. 'I like Caboyea,' she protested. 'Their cabbies are polite fellows. No cheek, no sass. And why must I stay off Caboyea when it's you who...who...your...whose...oh hell, I don't know what I'm trying to say.'

Aditi wagged a finger slowly in the other girl's face. 'It's a matter of principle. No Caboyea,' she pronounced owlishly. And they duly called another cab service when it was time to go home.

~

The new pattern didn't stay the course. Aditi tried to drown her sorrows, heartbreak she called it when she was a few drinks down, for a few evenings more but quickly called a halt to proceedings. Not only did it just not work, it interfered with her being in top form at office the next day. This was a double whammy; she'd socialize like mad, drink like crazy, come home and sit up all night composing long, rambling and mostly incoherent messages to Aditya, which she would then quickly delete. Luckily, she didn't press 'send' on any. A couple of times, she drunk-dialled him but his phone was switched off, so presumably he was still abroad. Or so she told herself.

Her post-proposal plan was clearly failing. How on earth could a girl continue to cling like a limpet to a man who just wasn't available for her to do so?

After a night of frenetic unsent activity on her phone, the next day she felt like death warmed up at work, unable to think clearly, with a buzzing headache and a foggy brain. So being a sensible girl at heart, she decided she had no choice but to get over Aditya Shenoy. There was no getting around one fact: Op Stalk Him was going nowhere and it was time to drop it. She really hadn't thought the chiselled-jawed love of her life would just go off her like this. Cold turkey, damn the man.

The *Steel Flyover Beda* protest was scheduled for the coming Sunday and Aditi kept herself busy with her activist friends, arranging for banners, pennants and drumming up presence at the venue.

Sunday dawned bright and shining and Ritu, Mickey, Minu and Aditi caught a train to the Cubbon Park Metro station, then walked over to where the protest was to start. It was just past 8 a.m., but the crowds had started to build and so had the heat.

This was to be a silent protest, just a long, snaking line of people who opposed the construction of the massive steel flyover which would involve the hacking down of as many as a thousand trees, all along the route of the proposed monstrosity. As for the benefits of both the flyover and the protest, the jury was still out on that.

Mickey was back on his hobby horse. 'Why on earth are we being so civilized about this?' he grumbled. 'We need a loud, violent protest to grab the attention of such a shameless government. We need to picket the CM's house, throw some stones…stuff like that!'

Ritu looked quite taken with the idea of them throwing stones while Minu looked distinctly alarmed. 'Are you mad?' Aditi asked him tartly. 'We don't do violent destructive protests in these parts. In any case, that would thwart the very goal of the protests. We need to reveal our numbers, our show of strength. After which, we will tackle the legal aspects and see how next to stop these people.'

Mickey continued to look unconvinced. Just at that moment, a suave politician from the opposition party walked by, palms together, officiously thanking them for being there.

'See?' Mickey hissed. 'They are hijacking the show. They are now pretending *they* set up this protest!'

'Pols will be pols,' Ritu pronounced sagely, pulling out a floppy hat and plopping it onto her head. 'I read somewhere this morning that the Bangalorean's true strength lies in their pragmatism. We need to work pragmatically to get results.'

Aditi stared at her friend. 'That's pure bakwaas!' she exclaimed. 'What does that even mean?'

Ritu opened her mouth to answer but was interrupted by Minu. 'Look!' Minu said, pointing to a spot up the road. They looked and saw a clutch of local film starlets a hundred yards away, pulling on fedoras, applying sunscreen and waving gracefully to the slowly cruising OB vans. Aditi chuckled and said, 'Well, they have turned up, haven't they? So they support the cause.'

The morning grew steadily hotter but the protest was due to break up in another hour's time. All the usual suspects had fetched up: filmstars, theatrepeople, socialites, politicians of the opposition parties and a handful of big businessmen and women.

'Whoever heard of a two-hour protest?' grumbled Mickey, still harping on the old theme. 'This protest lacks teeth!'

Despite knowing better, Aditi picked up the gauntlet. 'How come you were all for those silent protests when they were doing it in Istanbul? It worked there, na?'

'Actually, it didn't,' Mickey informed her and they fell to some minutes of aimless squabbling.

'Where's Sudarshan Kamath?' Ritu asked suddenly, for the moment forgetting that Aditi had dated the man's son.

Mickey snorted. 'Oh, he won't be here,' he announced.

All eyes turned to him enquiringly.

'Don't you guys read the papers?' he asked with some asperity. 'Sudarshan Kamath is bidding to supply steel for the very flyover we are protesting!' he finished with a flourish.

'Ah, that is just what Sudarshan Kamath would do,' Ritu said. 'Which is probably why his son isn't here either.'

Before she could stop herself, Aditi blurted out, 'If you mean Aditya, he's abroad.'

'No, he's not,' retorted Ritu. 'He was asked about this protest and he said he steered clear of political matters.'

'He did not!' mouthed a shocked Aditi.

'He did too!' said Ritu. 'It was awful to hear him.' She caught Aditi's eye and said, 'Last evening. On prime-time TV.'

'He was just playing safe,' Mickey said, his face carefully expressionless.

Aditi felt impelled to protest. 'Not to save Sudarshan Kamath's skin, you guys,' she told them. 'He's in talks with some Canadian company and is possibly playing safe so that the deal can go through.'

Before he could stop himself, Mickey said, 'And that makes it better?' then looked contrite. The others kept a telling silence. His non-appearance made Aditya Shenoy look bad and there was no way around that.

By 10 a.m., the lines broke up, people congratulated each other and went off. Some of Mickey's cynicism had rubbed off on Aditi and she felt dispirited. Would anything really come of this polite protest? They had turned up in huge numbers yes, but the authorities were a shameless, opportunistic lot. Would the city's residents keep up the pressure? Time would tell.

Just about all of the protesters converged on the city's popular breakfast joints in the vicinity, at Veena Stores, CTR, MTR, to close the protest with 'tiffin'. The queues outside these joints snaked quite like the Steel Flyover Beda line but eventually Aditi and her friends managed a table at CTR and started to wolf down *benne dosai* like there was no tomorrow. Obviously protesting, even protesting politely, was hungry work.

Quite like someone worrying a sore tooth, Aditi had to ask, 'What did Sudarshan Kamath have to say about the protest, though?'

Her friends exchanged glances, then Mickey complied. 'He said it was just a small amount of the population who were organizing this "impractical" protest. That the flyover would put us on par with...'

'...don't tell me, European cities?' groaned Ritu.

Mickey nodded. 'European cities,' he pronounced, his voice laced with sarcasm.

'Idiots!' Ritu ground out through gritted teeth. 'The flyover bridges they talk about in Europe all span rivers. This one will loom over buildings on the arterial roads of the city. They should be looking at a better bus system, a better Metro network.'

But Aditi was still chugging along another track. 'And what did Aditya Shenoy have to say?'

Her friends exchanged very speaking glances this time.

'They caught him as he was coming out of work, peppered him with questions about his relationship with his father, Caboyea's plans for the future and then, almost in passing, asked him if he was joining the *Steel Floyover Beda* protest,' Ritu told her. 'He said no, he never got involved in political protests. And that was all he would say. Then he went off.'

'But is this a political protest?' Aditi asked them. Nobody bothered to reply.

To be fair to him, he had never been keen on the protest but it bothered her that he hadn't joined in; now, it looked as if he was staying away because of his father's involvement. She would ask him the very next time she saw him, she decided, forgetting for one happy moment that she just didn't see him these days. Then memory came rushing back and she felt low again.

CHAPTER TWELVE

Enough with this ghosting, Aditi decided on a note of irritation. She needed to know where the relationship stood, and for that, they just had to meet. This time she would keep at it till she got through to him and she wouldn't take no for an answer, she resolved, and rang him repeatedly. He finally answered, on the third attempt, the second day. Tamping down a flare of anger at the way he seemed to be playing with her, Aditi kept her voice pleasant.

'Hi Aditya, wassup?'

The ensuing silence revealed that he was taken aback by her cheerful tone.

'Hi Aditi, all good. Tell me…?'

She just had to laugh; this was the standard response by Bangaloreans when you called them.

But she decided to play it as it went. 'Okay,' she chirped. 'I'll tell you. I called to ask if we could meet…?'

There was another beat of silence. Even as she screwed her eyes shut in anticipation of a rejection, he said cautiously, 'Okay. When?'

Aditi blanked out for a moment with sheer relief. She had really thought he'd say no. When the silence went on, he asked uncertainly, 'Aditi…?'

'I'm here,' she replied. 'Let's grab a coffee this evening, if you are free? Thre's a new roastery on Lavelle Road…'

'Yup, I know it. The guy who owns the place, Divakar, is a friend. I'll see you there.'

She didn't get a chance to rush off home and change after work but on second thoughts maybe that was good. She didn't want to go there all dressed up. Who knew how it would go? She didn't want to get high on hope, either.

Meeting A this evening for coffee, she texted Ritu.

And got an immediate reply. **Wotz the plan?**

No plan she texted back. Which must have foxed Ritu because that kind of shut down the conversation.

Aditya was already seated at a table when she walked into the light-filled, airy café. Her eyes drank him in hungrily even as she pinned on a bright smile. He looked gorgeous but there was a wary look in his eyes that she recognized.

He stood up formally but she wasn't going to settle for that; she went up to him and gave him a warm hug. It felt so good to have her arms around him again but she was careful not to prolong the moment or the hug.

He'd already ordered a house-special dark, she settled for a pumpkin spice latte, and they made painful small talk while waiting for their coffees. Divakar came over and Aditya introduced them. She registered that he told Divakar that she was his 'good friend,' and tried not to let that matter.

'Do you want a snack to have with your coffee?' he asked, pushing the wooden menuboard towards her, after Divakar had left them.

'Nope,' she said, grinning. 'I've been scarfing down doughnuts all day! Can't afford to put on more weight.' And she cocked her head like a robin, waiting for him to say something about her figure.

He didn't. He smiled a smile that didn't reach his eyes and replapsed into silence.

Oh shoot. This wasn't going to go easy.

And on the heels of that thought, she decided to stop pussyfooting and come down to brass tacks.

'Aditya,' she said earnestly, leaning forward. 'Are we really through?'

For a moment a very male look of horror crossed his face. He clearly didn't want to dissect their relationship or their break-up.

She didn't say anything more, just watched him intently.

He ran a hand through his hair, then down the side of his jaw. He looked up at her and caught the expression in her eyes, and suddenly all his barriers came down.

'Aditi,' he said fiercely, reaching for her hand. '*You* tell me if we are through.'

Navigating the bramble bush that had suddenly sprung up in front of her, she said carefully, adopting a neutral tone, 'Well, you were the one who dumped me, isn't it?'

'Oh for heaven's sake,' he ground out exasperatedly. 'Of course I didn't dump you!'

'Then why are we not seeing each other any more?' she asked him directly.

For a moment, it looked as if he was going to fob her off with some excuse about work. But once again, he looked into her eyes and seemed to change his mind.

Aditya then took a deep breath. 'Will you marry me?' he asked, hope and cycnicism twined together in that question.

It was Aditi's turn to take a deep breath. 'Does our future relationship hinge on my answer, Aditya?'

'Yes. Because otherwise, much as we care for each other, both of us are wasting our time. We are looking for different things in a relationship and being together will just twist the knife in deeper.'

Even as his tone was firm, even adamant, his eyes were entreating, literally begging her to give him the answer he wanted.

But Aditi Pillai wasn't going to lie, not to him, not about something which mattered so much to her.

She sighed and it was as if a guttering candle had just been blown out.

'Aditya Shenoy,' she told him, her voice calm, her gaze steady. 'I'm crazy about you and you know that. We are in a committed relationship, or were, if you'd rather have it that way. But I will not marry you just because you are setting that as a precondition to a future together.'

Their coffees came and he let go of her hand, slowly, reluctantly.

Striving for some equanimity, she reached out, picked up the coffee cup and had a sip. But that was all she could manage; her crazy emotions were threatening to overcome her. Strangely enough, it wasn't so much despair that she felt right now as a cold anger.

Looking straight at him, she said, 'That then, is that. There's nothing left to say, isn't it?'

'Have you thought this through at all?' he asked her, a frustrated edge in his voice.

She sparked with anger. 'Of course I have, dammit. You think my reply was on a bloody whim? I could easily tell you I've changed my mind, that I'm ready to marry you and we'd get back on track. But that would be cheating you, cheating myself. At the first sign of trouble ahead, both of us would use that very point to bludgeon each other, and you know it.'

Aditya had recovered his poise and continued to drink his

coffee with infuriating calmness, even though she knew he was just better at acting than she was.

'Why?' she burst out suddenly and he looked up startled. 'Why on earth are you so fixated on that meaningless marriage certificate? Why can't we just go on as we are for a bit longer, test-drive our relationship, see if one of us will change their mind?'

He smiled a sad smile. 'I would do that in a heartbeat, Aditi, you know that. I can't begin to tell you my current state of mind. Life is so bleak without you. But you know and I know that we are not on the same page here. Staying together would be pointless.'

Her pride reasserted itself at this point though she had never felt more bombed out.

'You know what? I'm done with this coffee and this conversation,' she told him, a bitter twist to her lips. 'See you when I see you.'

And she walked out of the café, out of his life, telling herself afresh that Aditya Shenoy just didn't deserve her.

So. Aditi Pillai had turned him down. Then he had turned her down. They were quits. And rather than be crushed by the blow of a failed relationship, she decided to fuel her determination with anger. She got up the next morning and told herself: *I'm so over Aditya Shenoy.*

At first, it was deceptively easy. She picked up her life-before-Aditya, hitting all the usual miniplexes, clubs and restaurants with the usual suspects. Only now everywhere she went, there was a touch of Aditya...in the decor (he liked this place/loathed that place) the food (this was his favourite dish/that one he detested), the music (every time they played trance someplace, she winced both for herself and for him). She found herself staring hard at people with faintly familiar profiles, only to suffer a pang of disappointment when they weren't him. Her ears pricked up at the deep sound of a Ducati weaving in and out of traffic, coming to a smooth stop, starting up powerfully; she hadn't realized there were quite so many machines of that make in town.

'Dammit!' she burst out to Ritu one evening. 'How can Bangalore be big enough for him and me to not meet each other?'

Ritu looked sympathetic. 'How long has it been since the two of you broke up?' she asked.

Offended by the question, Aditi glared at her. 'Going on two months,' then added fiercely, 'but it was not a formal break-up. We were...' Here she trailed off and Ritu interjected helpfully, 'Taking a break?'

'Yes,' Aditi agreed. 'Taking a break.' Her eyes met Ritu's and she grimaced. 'That's crap. I guess I'm still in denial. I just can't believe that Aditya Shenoy has given up on me like this.'

Ritu fixed her with a direct look. 'Would you have changed your mind about marrying him if he continued to see you and kept bringing the topic up?'

Aditi shook her head. 'No,' she admitted.

Ritu went to being her philosophical best. 'Give it time,' she advised. 'Either you will get over the dude. Or he will come back to you.'

~

Some days later, Ritu and she were at a new coastal restaurant in Indiranagar and were quite delighted at their impulsive decision to walk in here. The food was delicious, all of it. There were only two other tables which were occupied and the diners were quietly relishing the food. Wooden utensils hung from the walls, there were rice pounders with pestles, wooden kitchen stools and other utensils from another time in various corners of the large room, and one wall had alcoves with small lit lamps in them, all making for a very attractive ambience.

The peaceful lull was briefly broken when a large party of diners entered and were shown to their table. Aditi registered that there was an assortment of men, women and children in the group before her eye was caught and held by Amma. Amma, Preetha, Raj were there; the rest were unknown to Aditi. No Aditya, however.

Uncertain whether to smile or look away, Aditi continued to look at Amma. The older woman raised a hand in greeting and Aditi broke into a relieved smile.

'Who is that?' asked a curious Ritu, turning to follow Aditi's line of sight.

'Shakunthala Shenoy. The former Mrs Kamath…Aditya's mother,' Aditi told her.

'Wow, she's lovely,' breathed Ritu. Aditi nodded. This evening, Amma had on a tussar silk sari draped most gracefully across her slender form. The group seated themselves and started chatting, the children running around the table excitedly. Amma told Preetha something and the woman turned sharply in her seat to look at Aditi. Aditi smiled but Preetha continued to stare, then turned back.

Aditi swore softly but fluently, her string of colourful invective bringing on a fit of the giggles in Ritu.

'What?' asked Ritu eventually sobering up.

'Gosh, I feel so snubbed,' Aditi said. 'Preetha just cut me dead. Such a weird woman, I tell you.'

'Well, she would, wouldn't she?' asked an irritatingly practical Ritu.

'You mean Aditya would have told her we broke up? And why we broke up?'

The girls came to the end of their meal. 'Dessert?' asked Ritu and Aditi shook her head. 'I just want to get outta here,' she said.

'Rubbish!' Ritu said, 'I want to try dessert. Their food is so good, let's see how their sweets fare in comparison.'

Aditi glared frustratedly at her friend who blithely tuned her out and after a detailed perusal of the menu, settled for a coconut soufflé. When it arrived, Ritu dug a spoon in, took a mouthful and sighed in bliss.

'This. Is. Divine,' she pronounced dramatically, proffering a spoonful to Aditi. Aditi tasted the pudding and found Ritu had not been exaggerating. The soufflé melted on the tongue in a most satisfying manner.

They had called for the bill when she saw Amma wend her way, presumably to the Ladies' Room.

'Let's go,' she told Ritu in a low voice, 'Amma is going to the loo...' and then she trailed off because Amma had altered the course of her path and was bearing down on them. She came up to the girls' table and smiled down at Aditi. She immediately got up and made the introductions.

'Ah yes, Ritu,' Amma said on an easy note. 'I've heard about you from Aditya.'

At which Ritu, the traitor, mumbled something and made for the Ladies' Room herself, leaving Aditi alone with Amma. Aditi felt a momentary pang of nerves, then her natural self-confidence reasserted itself.

'How have you been, Aditi?' Amma asked her kindly.

'I've been good,' Aditi said then asked about her health.

From there, they got to praising the food at the restaurant.

'It's good, hearty Mangalorean fare,' Amma told Aditi with a wry smile. 'Very hard to pull off actually because of the simplicity required. But these people have managed to do it. I really liked their fish pulimunchi.'

'Have you got to the desserts yet?' Aditi asked and received a shake of the head in reply. 'Well then, do try the coconut soufflé, it's one of the best I've had.' Then she remembered where she had eaten coconut soufflé last and hurriedly added, 'As good as yours!'

Amma laughed. 'You mean as good as Radha's. She makes an excellent coconut soufflé. It's one of Aditya's favourite sweets…'

Then she threw an enquiring look at the younger girl and said, 'You probably don't get to see much of him these days, do you?'

Aditi froze, then realized it was more a statement than a question and gave a rather uncomfortable smile in response.

Amma continued, 'These are bad days for Aditya. He's working eighteen-hour days and tells me he's yet to see any results…'

At this point, she caught the surprised look in Aditi's eyes and paused, then exclaimed, 'Oh! You don't know? He didn't tell you? The Canadians are finding our regulations too restrictive, they don't want to sign on. If they do, they want some major restructuring, which Aditya doesn't want. Given that it was really a good deal for Caboyea, he's fighting tooth and nail to keep them interested. It's all touch-and-go, though.'

Then she looked straight at Aditi and asked, 'But why hasn't he told you all this himself? Don't you and he talk about your respective work?'

Aditi took a deep breath. This lovely woman deserves to know the truth, she decided. 'Amma, Aditya and I have broken up,' she said her tone faltering but her gaze steady.

It was clear that Amma hadn't known. She was visibly taken aback. Then gently but firmly, she asked, 'But why?'

Aditi really didn't know what to say to that. Even as she

hesitated, Ritu returned to the table. Amma leaned forward and took Aditi's hand. 'Aditi, you are the best thing that has happened to my Aditya for a long time. Whatever the problem is, talk it out with him. Maybe not now, though…the poor boy's got his hands full at the moment.'

And with a gracious smile, she went her way, leaving both the girls staring at her retreating back: Ritu admiringly, Aditi in a conflicted fashion.

'Why does Aditya have his hands full at the moment?' Ritu demanded to know and Aditi told her what she'd heard from Amma.

I'll call him again once I'm home, she resolved. Just to chat. *He needs to relax, loosen up, just share a laugh. Even if it's with his ex-girlfriend.*

Except, she never got to go home early that night. Just as they got off the Metro at Indiranagar and looked for an auto to go home in, Aditi's phone rang. It was Anita.

For a minute she was too surprised by the fact that Anita had called her outside working hours to react. Then she realized that the girl was in tears and sharply asked, 'What is it, Anita?'

The story emerged in between sobs and it concerned Bobby. Apparently, their gang of four friends had gone pubbing and since it was well past eleven and they had been drinking, they had called for a cab to take them home.

'The cabbie was drunk, the whole cab smelled of liquor. We should have got out then. Then he turned abusive and got into a scrap with Bobby and Srini,' Anita told her. 'He stopped the car and the three got into a fight. Bobby knocked the driver out. We don't want to call the cops,' Anita wailed, coming to the end of her story.

'Stay there,' Aditi instructed her tersely, after getting the coordinates. Ritu wanted to come along but Aditi sent her off and took an auto to where Anita and the rest of them were. It was merely two kilometres away but on a deserted stretch that ran parallel to Old Airport Road. Was it a Caboyea car, she wondered.

It wasn't, it was a cab belonging to one of the big aggregators. The cabbie was indeed out but Aditi, feigning a calm efficiency which she did not feel, searched for the man's pulse and found it; he had just been knocked out.

'Who hit him so hard? You?' She demanded incredulously of the skinny Bobby.

He looked less shamefaced and more proud as he said, 'Yes, I did. He was calling the girls names.'

Aditi took a deep breath. 'Alright, Bobby,' she said. 'But why didn't you take down his details, get out of the vehicle and head to the cops instead?'

Both the boys looked as if such a thought had not entered their heads. *Idiots*, Aditi thought. Thinking on her feet, she told the boys to head to the nearest paan shop or tea stall and get some water. 'Stop crying, Anita,' she told the girl who was snivelling along with the other girl beside her, Bobby's girlfriend presumably. 'There is nothing to cry about.' This brought on a fresh bout of tears in both the girls and Aditi sighed in exasperation.

Within the half-hour, the cabbie was up and belligerently ranting at them all. Switching to Kannada, Aditi put all efforts into calming him down. Ultimately, he subsided, sullenly grumbling and saying he would have to be paid handsomely if he wasn't to create a ruckus at the nearest police station.

Something snapped and Aditi straightened up, glaring at him. 'Yenappa?' she demanded stridently, and the man looked up, startled. 'You are going to file a police complaint? You? No! *We* are going to file a police complaint. You were harassing two women at this late hour.'

The man burst into protest. 'No, I wasn't! I was driving them home when suddenly the boys started abusing me,' and indicating Bobby, 'this fellow caught my collar from the back. While I was driving!'

'Don't talk rubbish,' Aditi told him, deliberately raising her voice. 'They told me all the facts. That you were grumbling from the moment they got into the cab. That you told them you'd drop them off halfway because you wanted to go off-duty. When they insisted you should drop them off at their destination, you turned abusive, started cursing, using bad language, made suggestive comments about the girls...' The girls were still sniffling and she pointed dramatically at them. 'See! You have traumatized the girls!'

The verbal face-off continued for a long while with the cabbie getting more belligerent by the minute. Bobby was of no help, none of the four were, Aditi realized, hampered as they were by a lack of Kannada, and possibly befuddled with drink.

But Aditi Pillai was not going to blink first, not with this cabbie. Suddenly, she changed tack and told everyone to get into the cab. After which she got in herself, squeezing herself onto the crowded back seat.

The cab driver stared at them. 'Get out of my cab,' he demanded.

'No. You are taking us to the police station,' Aditi told him calmly.

'No, I am not. Get out,' the man snarled.

'Well, if you are not taking us to the police station, I'm calling the cops here,' Aditi told him, taking out her mobile phone. 'Harassing women at night is a serious crime. It should be reported.'

Even as she quailed at the prospect of another stand-off with this nasty man, he capitulated suddenly. Going quiet as a mouse, he drove them to the nearest auto rank, where the four of them dispersed under Aditi's gimlet eye. She was beginning to feel like a vigilant aunt. Before they left, she made Bobby apologize to the cabbie. Just after they finished shaking hands reluctantly, the cabbie openly sneering, took a swipe at Bobby. Bobby ducked but the blow fell on his shoulder and his friend Srini moved to intervene. *Another fight?* Aditi thought in dismay, then quickly stepped in, and faced the cabbie down sternly, asking him, 'Do you really want a police case? Come on then, you'll get one!' Cursing below his breath, the man moved off, got into his cab and drove away.

'You, young man,' she told Bobby grimly, 'are more trouble than you are worth!'

He looked stricken at that but she refused to relent. 'We'll talk tomorrow,' she told him, then took an auto home, telling herself grimly that she needed to get herself a car. It was high time. She was getting tired of taking cabs or jostling for space on the now very crowded Metro runs.

~

The next morning dawned bright and she woke up with just one thought: she needed to get back in touch, and she meant real touch, with Aditya Shenoy. The simple truth was, they cared too much to just ignore each other's existence. Pulling on a canary-yellow crinkled-cotton skirt and a white tee, she walked into the living room and Ritu looked up from the newspaper. It was only then that Aditi caught the air of barely suppressed excitement in the room.

'You'll never guess who has made the front page today!' Ritu exclaimed.

Her mind still on her boyfriend, Aditi mouthed, 'Aditya Shenoy?'

'His father!' the other girl said. 'There was an ED raid on his Bangalore residence last evening…and he's flown the coop this morning!'

'Flown the coop?' Aditi asked, squinching her eyes. This was a complicated story but she was interested only in how it would impact Sudarshan Kamath's younger son.

'Yup,' pronounced Ritu, her voice still pitched high.

'Gimme the paper and stop acting like Arnab Goswami,' Aditi instructed her and pulled the paper towards herself. It was just as Ritu had told her. The enforcement directorate people had conducted a series of extended searches at all of Sudarshan Kamath's Bangalore properties; the report did not say what they had unearthed. But it did state that Kamath had caught the late-night flight to London, passing through Customs and Immigration unmolested. This was not surprising, though, since no charges had been filed against the man as yet. Watch this space, the newspaper stated gleefully.

And of course Aditi was not able to get through to Aditya Shenoy all of that day, try as hard as she could. He had apparently gone to ground, mainly to ward off the media. The media, undeterred and brash as ever, had gone chasing sound-bytes from Sudarshan Kamath's uncle in Udupi, and the man had flatly stated that he had not been in touch with his nephew for over a decade now. They then rushed to Shakunthala Kamath, and Aditi watched Amma ward off the ravening hordes with studied nonchalance, pretty much repeating what Kamath's uncle had said, but adding for good measure that it had been many, many years since she had laid eyes on her former husband. Raj and Preetha stood beside her and issued terse 'no comments' when they were approached. 'What a good-looking family,' one foolish young thing commented as part of her news report. The London reps of the bigger papers and television networks tried to get in touch with Sudarshan Kamath's second wife but she set her dogs on them, refusing to even emerge from her plush apartments in Kensington.

'Where is Aditya Kamath?' A TV news anchor blared like some sort of a foghorn. 'I'd like to know that too,' Aditi told him silently, trying to quell a surge of despair.

The days that followed brought only more news after sensational news. Sudarshan Kamath had extensive properties scattered over the globe and the manor house in London was a particular favourite; it was speculated that he would stay put there for the foreseeable future. What was galling for the authorities back home was that the man moved about in plain sight, no hiding or lying low for him.

'All this will be sorted out soon and I'll go back home,' he told the press, his collar turned up in a dashing manner against the bitter cold of a London winter.

'Who is handling your businesses back in India?' one reporter asked him and Aditi tensed. Despite everything that Aditya had told her, she still did not know the extent of his involvement in his father's affairs.

Sudarshan Kamath smiled a smile full of charm and grace. 'My businesses run like clockwork. I have very efficient managers and COOs who are handling everything…only till I return and take over again, you understand.'

In office, Mickey snorted and said, 'Of course, his businesses will run like clockwork. He has so many ties with so many important people that no one will touch his enterprises. Not until the heat is turned up, and I don't see that happening anytime soon.'

'Why?' asked Pia, a frown marring her pretty brow.

'Because Kamath's reach extends across the country,' Mickey dryly informed her.

Pia turned to a silently listening Aditi and said, 'Sorry, Addy.'

She raised an eyebrow at Pia, then laughed. 'Don't apologize, Pia,' she reassured the other girl. 'I'm not related to Sudarshan Kamath.'

Pia opened her mouth to say something in reply but Raman hastily stepped in and changed the subject. Mickey gave Aditi a severe talking-to for not calling him to handle the fracas of the previous night, then proceeded to give both the cringing interns a solid shelling. Anita stood, head down, silently absorbing whatever the big boss had to say. Bobby fidgeted, then looked up, caught Aditi's eye and had the gall to throw her a wink.

Bloody hell, thought Aditi, *the sooner that guy finishes his stint here, the better.*

'I'm so worried, I'm slowly going out of my mind,' Aditi confided in Mickey and Minu later that evening at their place. 'I spoke to Amma this afternoon. She told me the IT people had conducted raids at their place too, not that they found anything. She is sure Aditya has been raided too.'

'You didn't...' Mickey began to ask but she forestalled him saying, 'I did. I asked about Aditya. He's in Chikmagalur, at his cousin's coffee estates.' A dejected look came on her face and both Mickey and Minu looked away, their hearts wrung. 'Amma said he would surely take my calls. But he isn't doing so. And I don't know what to do.'

'Give him some time, Addy,' Mickey advised gently and awkwardly. 'He needs to sort all this out first.'

Aditi knew that to be true. Aditya *did* have a lot on his plate. Sudarshan Kamath's fleeing the country was more than just an embarrassment to him. After all, he had told her he was going to make Sudarshan Kamath give Raj his rightful place as eldest son in his will. That didn't look like it was going to happen now.

She felt a pang at the thought that Aditya was facing these extremely stressful times on his own. Oh, he had Amma, Preetha and maybe Raj too, though she didn't see Raj being of any conceivable help to Aditya. But she, Aditi, had been closer than this to him, and she should have been with him. The thought then crept into her head that she *would* have been with him if she had accepted his proposal, and she brushed the thought away. This was not an either/or situation.

Aditya was a decent man who went quietly about his life, ran a business on straight lines, played with a straight bat, steered clear of unethical practices. It was such a damned shame that life constantly put him in spots he had to work his way out of.

One thing she was certain about, though. She loved-loved-loved Aditya Shenoy, she wanted to spend the rest of her life with him and nothing else mattered. Now if she only got a chance to meet him and tell him that. And tell him other things, too.

What she got instead, was a call from a web magazine. The chirpy, very young voice at the other end said, 'Aditi Pillai? As Aditya Kamath's girlfriend, what do you have to say about the recent scandal? Is Aditya going to run his father's businesses for him in his stead?'

For a second, Aditi was speechless with outrage. Then she recovered her wits and asked the reporter acidly, 'Who told you I'm Aditya's girlfriend?'

Unabashed, the voice at the other end shot back, 'Our society photographer has snaps of the two of you taken over many months. Are you going to deny that you are Aditya Kamath's girlfriend?'

Aditi thought for a moment, then took a deep breath. 'I am

neither denying nor accepting anything you say. But first, get your facts right: he is Aditya Shenoy, not Aditya Kamath.'

'Okay, whatever,' the reporter said in a careless tone, 'But what is your take…?'

'I don't have any take, as you call it, since this matter doesn't concern me at all,' Aditi informed her and clicked off.

Late in the night, she wandered barefoot into Ritu's bedroom. Ritu was watching a Salman Khan film and thoroughly relishing it but she obediently pressed the pause button and looked enquiringly at Aditi.

'Should I marry Aditya?' Aditi asked Ritu.

To her credit, Ritu didn't evade that tricky question. 'No. Not because you are feeling wretched about the situation he is in. That's no reason to get married.'

'In that case,' Aditi burst out, 'I have no reason to marry him.'

Ritu said, reasonably enough, 'In that case, don't marry him.'

'But I want him back in my life. For ever and ever. On his terms, if he won't accept my terms.'

Ritu sat up and hissed fiercely. 'Don't be stupid, Addy! That's the pathway to future unhappiness. Listen, just wait till you meet him next. Then take it up from where it lies…'

She pulled Aditi down onto the bed and proceeded to give her a half-hour's worth of earnest advice. But Aditi was feeling absolutely wretched. The only clear thought in her head was that she wanted to be with Aditya, come what may. If it took a wedding ring to achieve that togetherness, well, she'd suck up her beliefs, deep-seated though they were, and try to adjust to what he wanted. Except, this line of thinking was making her feel more depressed.

Eventually, Ritu realized her words were falling on deaf ears and let Aditi go.

CHAPTER THIRTEEN

It was just her bad luck that Aditi had to run into Preetha the very next day, when she was in such a fragile state of mind. She'd just finished a one-day training capsule for a set of home chefs they were about to take on board. These chefs were going to come onto the Snack Team's roster, and everyone concerned was looking forward to it. The training class had been held at an office off MG Road and she was briskly walking towards the nearest Metro station when a car pulled up beside her and a voice asked, 'Aditi? Can I give you a drop somewhere?'

Much as she wanted to reply, 'Nope, your brother-in-law has done a good enough job of dropping me,' Aditi turned to look at Preetha behind the wheel of her car and said, 'No thanks, I'm heading home.'

But Preetha wasn't to be fobbed off. 'Home being Tippasandra? I'm going to Indiranagar, I can drop you off at your place.'

Aditi felt her temper rise. However, she controlled herself and got into the car, flashing Preetha a perfunctory smile. She was a strong girl, she could take whatever Preetha was going to throw at her.

But Preetha was nothing if not subtle. She made desultory conversation for much of the journey and Aditi felt her jaw beginning to ache from the effort of not grinding her teeth. Damn the woman, what was she playing at? Enough was enough.

So she turned in her seat and asked, 'Is there something you want to talk to me about, Preetha? I mean, you've more or less forced me to get into this car, so you must have a motive.'

Preetha looked startled for a moment, then protested, 'Hey, do I need to have a motive? I thought we were friends.'

'Hardly,' Aditi riposted dryly. Let's have this out, she decided and said, 'Every time we meet, you are either sizing me up or warning me off your brother-in-law or cutting me dead...'

Typically, Preetha latched onto the last bit. 'When did I cut you dead?' she asked, her voice soft and pained.

'Oh, just the other evening at that restaurant in Indiranagar. When all of you had come for a family meal or something. Amma came over to talk to me. I didn't think you would do that but when I looked at you, you just looked away.'

An uncomfortable silence ensued but to Preetha's credit, she didn't try to deny what Aditi said.

After a minute, she asked Aditi, 'Shall we stop for coffee?'

'Again?' Aditi retorted before she could help herself. 'No thanks, I don't think we are destined to become coffee companions.'

Preetha sighed then gave her attention to a more than usually crowded Ulsoor Road. After a while she said quietly but with feeling, 'I just wanted to ask you why you have walked away from Aditya. I thought you two had a good thing going...'

'Is that what Aditya has told you? That I walked away from him?' She hoped to hell the sting of tears didn't reveal itself in her voice.

Preetha hesitated. 'Well, not in so many words but yes, that was what we understood, Amma and I. She had called and asked him to bring you over to the house again, just before...before my father-in-law fled the country.' She said the last bit in a matter-of-fact voice which didn't hide the emotion she was clearly feeling. Aditi felt sorry for all the Shenoys.

She drew a pained breath. 'You know what, Preetha, I really appreciate your concern for your brother-in-law, and I assure you I'm not taking this in the wrong way. But it's a private thing between Aditya and me. Yes, we have a problem. We have to sort it out. I think we will sort it out eventually. And that's all I can say at this point.'

The rest of the drive was accomplished in silence. They got onto Indiranagar's 80 Feet Road and on impulse, Aditi turned to Preetha and said, 'You can drop me off here, I will just hop into the office for a few minutes.'

As she got off and thanked Preetha very formally, the other woman looked at her and said, 'He is so low, Aditi. I have never seen him like this. And you don't look so good yourself...' This impacted Aditi more than anything else Preetha had said, a picture of Aditya entering her mind with sharp and jagged precision. She looked at Preetha, her eyes bright with the sheen of tears.

Preetha sighed. 'I was wrong to be so suspicious. You are really good for him. So go and sort out your issues, won't you? Go to his place...'

Aditi blinked away her tears and stared at Preetha. 'He's there at home?'

'Yes, he returned from Chikmagalur yesterday. I think he's got the foreign investor matter under control for the time being.' And for the first time since they met, Preetha actually smiled at Aditi, a friendly smile. Then she added, a sparkle coming into her eyes, 'You see, I'm rooting for team A-A.'

'Team A-A?' Aditi started to ask, then caught on and gave her a watery smile.

She was alone in the office and quite glad about that since she needed to think. Would it be okay if she just landed up at Aditya's door? Would he shut that door in her face? After all, he'd pretty much cut himself off from her in devastatingly effective fashion.

There was a piece of paper pinned onto their workboard and it said in large jubilant letters: THE FLYOVER BEDA PROTEST WORKED! PLANS FOR STEEL FLYOVER SCRAPPED! She stared at it, slowly taking in the meaning but unable to feel excited. She had a report to write about the training capsule and she tried to do that, shutting all thoughts of Aditya Shenoy from her head. That didn't turn out to be a successful endeavour, though, so she gave up the attempt and decided it was time to leave.

As she left the office, Aditi paused to look at herself in the mirror that hung in the tiny space that they grandly liked to call the foyer. *Nothing ventured, nothing gained, Aditi Pillai*, she told herself, aiming for a jaunty note and nearly getting there. Then she took herself off home.

~

Ritu wasn't at home and for once, Aditi was glad of that, too. This time she didn't want to ask anyone about what she was planning to do. In actual fact, she herself wasn't too sure what she was going to tell Aditya when she came face-to-face with him. She came to a quick decision: she was going to go with the flow, just take whatever came as it came.

But she was going to go dressed for the occasion. She wore a teal-coloured skirt, pulled on a silky jersey top the colour of her eyes and loaded herself with her silver jewellery. Hair up or down, she asked herself, then decided it was better up, so she scrunched her curls up in a high ponytail that threw her delicate features into flattering relief, and set off.

She called a Caboyea car, smiling at the young driver who looked disconcerted at first, then offered her a sweet smile of his own. In the car, she turned off her cellphone; she needed to think out what she was going to say, what she was going to do. If the phone was on, she'd either be checking stuff or sending impassioned pleas for advice to her gang. This time, she had to do what she had set out to do, on her own.

Within forty minutes, they had reached the head of Richmond Road, where they then proceeded to stay stuck in traffic for a horrific forty minutes. Even this late in the evening, cars were trapped bumper to bumper, tempers were running high, the air was rent with the sound of blaring horns and the fact that the kerbside was dug up for heaven knew what added to the general misery. This then, was just another typical Bangalore evening, and Aditi fumed in silence.

At any other time, she would have engaged the cabbie in conversation, something she did regularly these days whenever she took a cab. Even the most surly of drivers usually relented and became quite pleasant when you engaged them in conversation, treated them as fellow human beings doing their jobs, not human machines who drove you to wherever you wanted to go. But right now she was consumed by feverish impatience and actually contemplated getting off and walking. Only the fact that Aditya's apartment was nowhere within walking distance stopped her. She started drumming her fingers on the armrest and the cabbie's eye met hers in understanding in the rear-view mirror. She took her hand off the armrest and concentrated on some deep breathing.

It was close on 9.30 p.m., when the vehicle finally drew up outside his apartment block but Aditi was still riding an adrenaline high. She got off hurriedly and faced the next hurdle at the security cubicle. She didn't want them to ring and tell Aditya beforehand, so she started to tell the men inside the cubicle, 'Neevu...' before she realized both of them were from the north-east. Switching to Hindi, she gave Aditya's name and apartment number, said she was his fiancé, then summoned up a coy smile and said, *'Unko mat bolna ki main aa rahi hoon.'* It was touch and go for a minute, then both the young men smiled and waved her through. Would their heads roll for this security breach she wondered, and took the same approach with the man who served as concierge in the lobby, and met with the same kind of success. Men, it seemed, were suckers for a good love story! Either that or she just didn't look like your average axe murderer.

She tried to calm herself in the silent, swift lift, staring blankly at her own reflection in the darkened mirrors on the four walls. Getting out, she walked towards Aditya's penthouse flat and raised her hand to press the doorbell, only to have it open in her face.

Aditya stood there in the doorway. She stared at him for one long moment, quickly registering two facts: he had lost weight and he had grown a beard. While the neatly trimmed beard cloaked that gorgeous jawline, it suited him she decided; he looked hot as hell. He was wearing a pair of faded jeans that fit him so sexily in all the right places, the sleeves of his shirt rolled up to just below his elbow, something she had insisted he do, telling him it was an instant turn-on. 'Oh, if it turns you on...' he had said with a mischievous grin, immediately rolling his sleeves up.

Even as she wondered if the security detail had called ahead and told him, she saw that he was as startled as she was. But he recovered quicker.

Smiling faintly, he told, 'Close your mouth, Aditi.' And she realized she had been gaping like a dimwitted fish. But dammit, she just couldn't help it, he looked so handsome and she was experiencing a breaking news moment: how much she had missed this man! She had missed his slow grin, his low-pitched laugh, that habit he had of snapping his fingers when he hit upon something, that molten look that came into his midnight dark eyes when he looked at her. She had missed the feel, the taste of his mouth on hers, the weight of his body on her, in her. She had missed Aditya Shenoy to hell and back. Now she was never going to let him go.

Stepping inside the apartment, she suddenly recovered her wits. 'Where were you off to?' she asked, inquisitively. She had caught a glimpse of his bike keys in his hand.

'To your place,' he told her with that slow smile of his, his teeth flashing white against the dark beard. 'I have been calling you for the last hour but your phone seems to be switched off. Is it? Switched off, I mean?'

Aditi's hand flew to her mouth. She had clean forgotten that she had switched off her phone and never once in that crawling traffic had she remembered to switch it back on.

His eyes crinkled with understanding and amusement. 'Then I tried Ritu. Who said you had some marathon training session planned for today and that you were going to come home late in all probability. I told her to see that you stayed home once you got home, and was just setting out to Tippasandra.'

He walked to the stone dish that contained all his keys and dropped his bike keys in there. Turning to her, he asked, 'Have you eaten?' When she shook her head, he asked, 'Shall we call in for food?'

Aditi squeezed her eyes shut for a second, then opened them. She hadn't come here to eat dinner.

'I'm not hungry,' she told him, and found her voice had gone all wonky.

His gaze locked on hers. 'Neither am I,' he told her seriously.

There was a moment of acutely conscious silence which they broke, speaking simultaneously.

'I…' began Aditi while he said, 'Aditi…'

He opened his mouth again but she forestalled him, raising a slender hand with unconscious grace.

'No, let me speak first, Aditya,' she told him and he nodded his head, indicating that they should sit down. Aditi ignored that, she needed to say her piece standing up.

'My anti-marriage stand? It's a personal thing. Very very personal,' she told him, fixing him with a level gaze. 'I have seen from up close what a bad marriage can do.'

He raised an enquiring eyebrow and she said, 'My parents.' Seeing the startled look in his eyes, she continued, 'Oh, they are together now. But for about five crucial years of my life, Ma, Akshay and me, we lived apart from Pa. Because Pa was having an affair with his secretary.' She gave a ghost of a laugh then continued. 'That old stereotype. It was tough going in the first two years or so but the three of us crafted some kind of life together, did our best to keep things normal. Ma took a job at our school. Akshay and I learned not to think too much about Pa. He was serving a stint abroad at that time so it was easier for us to hide the truth from people.

'Then Ma's family came and pressured us to return to Pa…after so many years! Pa had broken off his relationship with that woman and had promised his in-laws he wouldn't stray again. He had gone to them, begged and pleaded and they persuaded us to go back.

'But it devastated us, took the sunshine out of Ma's life forever, ensured that Akshay and I would grow up wary, insecure, always covering up that insecurity with forced gaiety. Ma didn't say one word against Pa in all these years but we were already young adults when the break-up happened, we had formed our opinions. And now we were to be back with him, to re-learn to love him, respect him. We would watch Ma and Pa being so polite, so formal with each other, and it took something out of us. All of us were play-acting. I hated it!'

She took a deep breath, then the words came rushing out again. 'And then, years later, Pa told me the woman was not his secretary. She was his childhood sweetheart, the woman he had always wanted to marry. His parents had forced him to marry Ma instead. Such a sham marriage. So much unhappiness all around. So much scarring all around.'

Aditya winced at the bitterness in her voice but continued to look intently at her.

'Pa never got over the guilt. Ma never got over the humiliation. And both Akshay and I grew up feeling nothing but contempt for the institution of marriage. And now, when Ma nags us to get married, Akshay and I don't know whether to laugh or cry!'

She swallowed hard, then continued. 'No one knows about this, Aditya. Not Ritu, not Mickey. Only you.'

'Thank you,' Aditya said and then she walked straight into his arms, hugging him tightly, burying her head in his chest. He could feel her slender form shaking, and he held her. They stood that way for a long time, then she raised her head.

'I haven't finished yet,' she told him, brushing the tears from her eyes impatiently.

'I have trust issues where marriage is concerned. I'm scarred, maybe for life, but I've had time to think long and hard on this issue. I really really love you, Aditya Shenoy,' she was speaking rapidly and slightly breathlessly but her gaze was steady. 'I love you to bits and I want you in my life forever and ever. If the only way I can have you is by marrying you, so be it. I'm not a domesticated animal but I'll try my best to be a good wife. I'll go for pre-marital counselling! Whatever it takes…let's get married!'

'Are you proposing to me, Aditi?' he asked, smiling, striving for an air of normalcy. What she had told him had put things in clear perspective. Both of them were products of less than happy marriages, yet he was seeking security in that very institution for himself while she was running away from formalized commitment.

She reached up and cupped the side of his face in her palm, and he drew in a sharp breath.

'Yes, I'm proposing to you,' she told him simply. 'Are you going to say yes?'

But he didn't. Still smiling, he drew her to him and bent his head purposefully. 'First things first, my dearest,' he told her in a very uneven voice, then kissed her. She slung both her arms around his neck, pulling him closer to her and returned the kiss with pent-up feeling. They kissed hard and long, putting everything they hadn't been able to talk about into the kiss, acknowledging everything she had told him. Then they moved apart and smiled at each other.

'Now, listen to me,' he told her, tenderly. 'I have a proposal for you.'

She raised an eyebrow at him. He put one hand to the back of her head and pulled off the elastic band that held her ponytail in place. As the curls cascaded down her shoulders and back, he ran a hand through them under her neck, saying 'It's been so long…'

Then he put her a little away from him and told her, 'It's been a hellish two-three months, Aditi. But it gave me a new insight into my life. And my life is worth zilch without you. It took me one hell of a long time to find you. And…' here he paused dramatically, 'If the only way I can have you is by agreeing not to marry you, so be it. Let's not get married!'

She stared at him and realized he meant every word. Aditi gave such a deep heartfelt sigh, her boyfriend started to laugh.

'We'll be together and that's the main thing. Are we going to be living together?' The last was asked casually but his eyes held a bit of tension. She nodded emphatically and he looked relieved.

He then said, 'My family will be relieved. They think this A is incomplete without the other A.'

She smiled and told him, 'Which is true.'

'We'll put in a water fountain if you want, like the one in your apartment,' he told her and looked at her in surprise when she threw her head back and cackled. When she got her breath back, she told him solemnly, 'In which case, I will not move in here with you. I detest that damned water fountain!'

'I hope you know one thing…' he said, cocking an eyebrow at her.

'What?' she asked.

'Well, apparently living together can work two ways. Either a relationship will achieve clarity and become even better or it will be pushed to its final closure. So say the experts.'

'Are you kidding?' Aditi asked, then told him clearly and precisely just what the experts could do with themselves, and he laughed out loud saying, 'Ah, I've missed that cussing of yours!'

She stuck her tongue out at him and said entirely unoffended, 'Yep. That's me.' A thought struck her and she added, 'I'll move in here but I'll keep the lease on the Tippasandra flat for one more year at least. I owe that much to Ritu.'

'I think that's a good idea,' he told her, a smile lurking deep in his dark eyes. She looked a question at him.

'I have this yen to make love to you on that yak-skin rug of yours, you see,' he told her conversationally. To her chagrin, she found herself going pink.

'Also, you get a bolt-hole every time you feel the need to run away from me, hmm?' he teased her, his hand exploring the soft skin at her collarbone.

'Well, of course I'll need that bolt-hole. What do you think, that you are god's gift to women?'

'I'm not?' he asked in mock disbelief and she made a moue.

'Well, maybe in bed...' she began provocatively and he took it up immediately, just as she hoped he would.

'Ah, in bed,' he said softly, cupping the back of her neck and gently drawing her into him. Bending his head, he trailed a series of kisses on the side of her neck. She shivered in delight but teased, 'Your beard scratches...'

He lifted his head. 'If you don't like it,' he told her, 'I'll shave it off. Tomorrow. For tonight, you will have to put up with it.'

And she did. Gladly and passionately. They made love like lovers who hadn't met for years. Their coming together was equal parts ravenous hunger and equal parts a delighted acknowledgement of their reconfigured relationship.

Much later, she asked him, 'Are you sure, Aditya?'

He didn't dissemble. Looking deep into her eyes, he said, 'Yes, I'm sure. I have my priorities set right now. And my priority is you, not marriage.'

She nodded, heaved a deep sigh then said, 'I get hyper in a second and then I say what comes to mind. Which usually gets me into hot water, very hot water. I also blurt out things on impulse, things I regret saying later on. But marriage is one thing I hold a definite opinion about. And now you know why.'

Looking away for a moment, she continued, 'At this point, I can't promise you anything. Except that I will be with you for the next sixty-odd years. Who knows, maybe I'll get over all my deep, dark fears of marriage and we can then formalize our relationship...'

'Yes,' he cut in with a deadpan expression, his eyes twinkling with merriment. 'On the twentieth anniversary of our being together. Or the thirtieth.'

She aimed a mock punch at his jaw, then leaned in to kiss him hard. Drawing away, she asked, 'How did the Canadian deal go?'

He leaned back against the headboard. 'They are still on board, as of now. I actually held some meetings at Chikmagalur with them. The POC keeps changing, given that this is a big step for them and for us. But I think they get the real picture now, that Caboyea doesn't promise the moon but definitely delivers on whatever it promises. I have a strong feeling that they will invest and stay invested but I'll know for sure only by next week.'

'Oh I hope so,' she told him. 'It must have been a rotten time...'

'Rotten doesn't begin to cover it,' he told her. 'I didn't want to divide my attention between my professional problems and my personal ones...'

'This is the first time I have been termed anyone's personal problem,' she interjected in protest. He grinned and replied, 'Well, there's no getting around that. You were. I wanted to sit down and sort out all the different chaotic thoughts inside my head. I was annoyed with you, exasperated, frustrated that you didn't see things my way. However, once I got things straight in my head, I knew I had to meet you, tell you what I feel. But that required time and I didn't have time at that point. So I decided to compartmentalize things, clinch the Canadian deal first if I could and then come to you on bended knees, to ask if you would come back to me, be mine forever, in whatever manner you wished.'

She stared at him, moved beyond words. He added, 'But I have to be honest. I had my father pegged as one of my personal problems, too.'

'Are you in touch with him?' she asked.

'Are you kidding?' he replied, with a twisted smile. 'I don't think my family or the country is going to see Sudarshan Kamath for a long while. I tried to apologize to Amma because I had promised her that Rajanna would get what was due to him from our father. She laughed and reminded me that they had, none of them, been very keen about this, that it had been some kind of obsession with me, about which they had just been humouring me.'

He pulled her closer to him and continued, 'In any case, it's not like they can't manage without my father's money. We are fairly comfortably placed, thank heaven.'

A contented silence prevailed but Aditi felt she needed to lighten things up. Adopting a ruminative tone, she asked him, 'What does "comfortably placed" mean? Are you wealthy? Seriously wealthy?'

'I'm never going to be seriously wealthy,' he began to tell her in a thoughtful tone, before he caught the glint of laughter in her eyes. Adopting a reflective tone to match hers, he then said, 'But I am not too sure. I'll need to sit with my CA on this.'

'Please do,' she told him switching to a fake, honeyed tone. 'I mean to live the rest of my days off you. That has always been my plan, to become a certified gold-digger from the moment I got to know you are more than just my cute cabbie!'

Aditya turned on his side to face her. 'Forget that plan. I have other plans for you,' he told her, one hand slipping beneath the sheets to cup her breast.

'You do?' she asked him, her breathing becoming erratic. 'What?'

'Let me show you,' he told her and proceeded to do just that.

Acknowledgements

My romance with romance novels continues and I'm hoping readers will enjoy reading this book as much as I enjoyed writing it.

Thank you Shyam Nair, enterprising entrepreneur, for giving me invaluable advice on my heroine's food start-up.

Thank you Jayanth Kodkani and Madhumati DS for patiently providing me with Kannada/Konkani words, terms, culinary details, as and when I needed them.

Thank you, Kelly and Sue, my Beta reader team…even though Sue struck me momentarily dumb with her Tharoor comparison. Those who want to know more will have to ask me in person!

Thank you Sudeshna Shome Ghosh, you've done a marvellous job of editing Aditi and Aditya's tale. Thank you Maithili Doshi for breathing life into the book cover.